Treat or Trick

Simon Fairbanks

To R. L. Stine for igniting my passion for
multiple-pathway stories.

To Charlie Brooker for reigniting that passion
twenty years later.

SIMON FAIRBANKS

Contents

Foreword

Bandersnatch.

A revolutionary episode of the dystopian television series *Black Mirror*.

Written by Charlie Brooker, and made possible by Netflix's technological know-how, Bandersnatch blew my mind. It took the multiple-pathway concept – a popular novel format – and reinvented it for the screen.

As I sat there, controlling the story with my remote control (or blipper, as my wife calls it), I was reminded of how much I loved reading multiple-pathway novels as a child, especially the *Give Yourself Goosebumps* series by R. L. Stine. Back then, I vowed to write my own one day. Now, with a few books under my belt, and propelled with fresh inspiration courtesy of Bandersnatch, it felt like the perfect time to revisit that vow.

In many ways, the multiple-pathway format is a

logical fit for me.

Firstly, it accommodates my passion for writing short stories because each pathway is essentially its own standalone story. You will find short pathways in *Treat or Trick*, not far off flash fiction, as well as longer novella-length pathways.

Secondly, the multiple-pathway approach fulfils my love of writing in different genres. As you delve into *Treat or Trick*, you could find yourself reading horror, crime, sci-fi, fantasy or a thriller, depending on the choices you make.

Finally, I am all about endings. I love crafting a story's resolution, labouring over the last sentence, deliberating on how best to deliver a twist. The multiple-pathway format allowed me to write twenty-six different endings. Pure joy.

I will talk more in the Afterword because, you know, spoilers, but suffice it to say that the whole experience of writing this book was deliriously good fun.

I hope you have as much fun reading it.

The ending is yours to decide.

Good luck.

Chapter 1

Jack couldn't be happier. He had taken his wife out earlier in the evening. Now that Joan was gone, he had the house all to himself.

Ding dong.

Except it was Halloween.

'Oh, come on.'

Joan had left a carved pumpkin in the bay window, lit up like a Christmas tree. The universal sign that a house was open for business.

Ding dong.

Jack longed for a quiet evening alone. He had already eaten half the treats set aside for the trick-or-treaters. Next, he planned to binge his way through his favourite horror show on Netflix. He would also have to clean the kitchen at some point too, but he was putting that off for as long as possible.

Ding dong.

Jack sighed. They weren't going away.

To answer the door, turn to page 5.

To leave the door unanswered, turn to page 7.

Chapter 2

'Trick or treat?'

Jack opened the door to find a trick-or-treater on his doorstep. He only recognised the youth as a trick-or-treater because he carried a plastic Aldi bag brimming with sweets.

The youth wore no mask or costume. The closest the boy had come to fancy dress was pulling up the hood on his sports-branded jumper.

Even so, Jack could still make out the youth's face. He was pushing the upper age limit for acceptable trick-or-treating. Jack suspected he was twelve, possibly on the brink of puberty, or just edging past it, judging by the whisper of hair on his lip.

'Mate,' said the youth, impatiently. 'Trick or treat?'

'Yes, sorry,' said Jack, waking up. 'Treat. Let me get you something. One second.'

To give him sugar, turn to page 10.

To give him fruit, turn to page 14.

Chapter 3

'Fuck that.'

Of course he wasn't going to answer the door.

What if the trick-or-treaters caught a whiff of the smell coming from the kitchen? What if they saw the blood under his fingernails, which he hadn't quite managed to scrub away?

But the ringing was enough to jolt him into finally cleaning the kitchen. He dragged himself away from the television and found the kitchen exactly as he left it.

'Hello Joan.'

Her body lay butchered on the tiled floor in a sopping wet pool of blood.

Jack had taken her out earlier in the evening, after learning of her affair with Ted. He confirmed his long-held suspicions by scrolling through her phone at a rare moment when it was both unattended and unlocked.

7

There had been an argument after that. Jack was known to get a little hot-headed whenever he found something vexing and his wife's infidelity was a pretty big something. Hot Head Jack. That had been his nickname at school. He loathed the name but, undeniably, the moniker was warranted tonight.

It was a short argument, at least. The moment Joan started comparing Jack and Ted as lovers, digging in the figurative knife with gleeful abandon, was the moment that Jack picked up the literal knife from the kitchen counter.

He stabbed her in the stomach.

And then some.

Now, looking at the mess, Jack huffed. 'Where do I even start?'

He sorely wished he had stabbed her just the once in a more efficient place. One quick thrust to the chest would have done the trick. Instead, he had gotten carried away, enjoyed himself, and now he had to pay for it with elbow grease.

Still, he should probably get rid of the body first. No sense in cleaning around it. Moving the damn thing would only cause more mess to leak out. Best to shift it before whacking out the Dettol.

'What shall I do with you?'

To cut up the body with a chainsaw, turn to page 16.
To burn the body in the back yard, turn to page 18.

Chapter 4

'Here, take it all.'

Jack emptied the bowl of chocolates and sweets into the teenager's Aldi bag. If they rotted his teeth, or their e-numbers sent him loopy for the rest of the evening, then that wasn't Jack's concern.

'Nice one, mate,' said the teenager, with a greedy grin. 'You just saved yourself an egging.'

'Good to know. Happy Halloween.'

Jack slammed the door in his face.

'Right.'

He marched straight to the lounge to remove the pumpkin from the bay window. He had no intention of entertaining any more trick-or-treaters this evening. Not that Joan needed to know that. He had emptied the bowl, so she would think he had been dishing out treats all night.

Ding dong.

'Damn it.'

Too slow. He abandoned the bay window and returned to the front door. These next trick-or-treaters were going to be disappointed.

Sorry kids, the last guy cleaned me out.

Jack opened the door –

'Trick or treat.'

– and jumped in alarm.

Three gruesome trick-or-treaters stood on his doorstep. They were smaller than the teenager, probably a more appropriate age for trick-or-treating, and they had put way more effort into their costumes.

The three kids wore matching black robes which stopped at the floor. Each carried a pumpkin, presumably hollowed-out for storing their treats. However, it was their masks which drew Jack's eye and had almost stopped his heart in fear.

No, not masks. More than that.

Left to right, he was looking at a jack-o'-lantern, skeleton and mummy.

The jack-o'-lantern appeared to be wearing an actual pumpkin as a mask, though Jack had no idea how the child was able to support its weight. He also couldn't make out any eyes through the carved, triangular eye holes. All he saw inside the pumpkin was a cluster of flickering flames, as though it contained no head at all. It was a nifty effect. Jack couldn't fathom how the kid was doing it.

The skeleton's head was an entire skull, not merely a plastic mask worn over the face. Like the jack-o'-lantern, Jack couldn't see any eyes looking out through the sockets. Jack assumed the kid was wearing a black morph suit underneath. For reasons unexplained, the skeleton was also wearing a jaunty top hat, as though dressed for a formal occasion. It reminded Jack of a joke: why didn't the skeleton go the ball?

And then there was the mummy costume, which was a claustrophobic panic attack waiting to happen. The whole child was tightly wrapped in filthy bandages, like they had genuinely climbed out of a sarcophagus after a thousand-year nap. The only reprieve from the bandages was a slit for the mouth – all the better for eating sweets – and an exposed area for the kid's eyes. The skin around the eyes was a triumph in make-up artistry. It was green and rotten like a two-day old avocado, whilst the eyeballs were bloodshot and jaundiced. The kid must have been wearing novelty contact lenses.

'Wow,' said Jack. 'Your parents really went to town on your costumes.'

'Trick or treat,' repeated the monsters, almost a growl.

'Yes, sorry, so you said. I'm all out of chocolates and sweets, I'm afraid.'

The three monsters exchanged urgent looks and chittered to each other in a language that Jack didn't understand. It was a multicultural neighbourhood, after all.

'*Trick* or treat?' they repeated.

Jack thought he heard an emphasis placed on the first word. Was that a threat?

'Alright, alright, alright,' said Jack. 'Don't worry. I'll find a treat for you.'

To give the monsters fruit, turn to page 22.

To give the monsters gum, turn to page 25.

Chapter 5

'Here you go.'

The trick-or-treater held out his plastic Aldi bag expectantly. Jack dropped an apple into it. There was no word of thanks, merely a stunned silence. The boy removed the apple from his bag in disgust.

'What the fuck is this?'

'It's an apple,' said Jack, already regretting the decision. 'They're good for you.'

'Good for me?'

'Full of vitamin C.'

'I didn't come here for vitamin C. It's Halloween.'

'Well, you'll be getting plenty of sugary stuff tonight,' said Jack. 'I thought an apple would be a welcome change.'

'You thought wrong. Halloween is about sweets and chocolate. Not apples.'

'People bob for apples on Halloween,' said Jack, standing his ground.

'I'll bob you, mate.'

'I'm sorry?'

'Trick time.'

The youth dropped his Aldi bag and delved both hands deep into the pockets of his hoody. His hands resurfaced holding eggs.

'Wait – ' began Jack.

The boy launched a volley of eggs at Jack, which splattered against his raised arms. Others sailed past him, making a mess of the walls and carpet of the exposed hallway behind him.

'Stop!' he pleaded.

'Or else what?' shouted the youth, readying another egg.

Show wrath, turn to page 28.

Show forgiveness, turn to page 31.

Chapter 6

Jack had once heard a saying which went, 'There are no big problems. Just a lot of little problems.' That saying had stuck with him ever since, so when he considered the bloody corpse of his dead wife, he knew exactly how to tackle the problem. He would simply break it up into lots of little pieces.

Jack went to get his chainsaw.

The chainsaw was his most unlikely possession. He had never owned such a thing before moving into his current house. Jack wasn't exactly a handy man. He was a call-a-guy guy. However, their house backed onto a wooded area, and the trees had been growing over their back fence when they first moved in. Something had to be done about it.

The chainsaw had solved that problem. The trees hadn't grown back since then, so the contraption sat dormant in the garage, forgotten, a waste of money.

But Jack was very thankful for the purchase now.

He didn't much fancy sawing through Joan's bones by hand. It would have taken ages. He still harboured the hope of returning to his Netflix show before the evening was over.

Jack pulled the cord.

By the time he was finished, the kitchen was messier than ever but the problem of the body itself was much more manageable. An arm, a calf, a chunk of torso – bite-sized pieces which he could stash in a bunch of different places. Easy.

It was only when the buzzing sound of the chainsaw subsided in his ears that he realised the door bell was ringing.

Ding dong.

Answer the door, turn to page 33.

Ignore the door, turn to page 36.

Chapter 7

A fire shouldn't cause too much suspicion. It was only a few more days until bonfire night and people were always burning random waste in their gardens at this time of year.

Jack and Joan lived at the end of a cul-de-sac – well, it was just Jack doing the living now – and only one neighbour could see into their garden. But that neighbour was Ivy, an octogenarian. Ivy would be in bed by now, dead to the world after removing her hearing aids. She wouldn't peek into Jack's garden tonight.

It was decided.

Fire.

'Well, Joan, you always wanted a cremation. I'll show you that courtesy at least.'

Building the pyre didn't take long at all. Jack's garden backed onto a wood, which he could access through a padlocked gate built into the fence at the top of the garden. A few foraging trips were enough to gather firewood for the pyre.

Starting the fire was much more troublesome. It was way harder than Jack remembered from his days as a cub scout. After numerous false starts, Jack resorted to watching a YouTube tutorial on his phone, and hated himself for it.

It's come to this, he lamented. *My generation can't even rub two sticks together without consulting the Internet.*

At least it got the fire going.

The hardest part was carrying Joan's body to the pyre. Jack didn't want Joan dripping all over the place on her journey from the kitchen, so he initially tried to shove her into a bin bag. But the bin bags were crappy things that tore easily. You get what you pay for at Aldi. After a failed triple-bagging attempt, Jack finally gave up in a huff.

Sod it. I have all night to clean.

Jack hoisted Joan into his arms – weirdly reminiscent of carrying her over the threshold after their wedding – and took her up the garden. It reminded Jack of the scene from *An Officer and a*

Gentleman, albeit an R-rated version with a dark, psychological twist.

It was a long walk but, thankfully, Joan was light as a feather. It surprised Jack until he remembered that most of her blood had been left behind on the kitchen floor.

During all of this activity – gathering wood, starting the fire, transporting Joan's body – Jack could hear his door bell ringing over and over again. Jack cursed the trick-or-treaters for not taking a hint. Kids were relentless in their quest for sugar.

I should have removed that damn pumpkin from the bay window.

He pictured the kids on his front doorstep, excited, laughing, dressed in their cute, plastic outfits. Most were probably dressed as Disney princesses or superheroes, instead of anything spooky.

Jack hated how commercial Halloween had become. It had been his favourite holiday as a child, back when it was about the ghosts and ghouls and scares. He had been fascinated by the idea that Halloween was the time of year when the fabric of the world grew thin and creatures could pass through from the other side.

But now Halloween was merely an excuse for toy companies to push their fancy dress items onto kids, and an excuse for kids to get a bucket-load of free chocolate.

If only they could see what is happening on this side of the house.

Then the kids would understand the true meaning of Halloween.

Fear, death, madness.

Jack grinned.

He pondered these thoughts whilst watching the flames course over Joan's body. It was a horrible sight, seeing his wife crisp and crackle and curl, but he felt a duty to observe. If you start something then you should finish it.

Besides, he was putting off the cleaning.

Turn to page 331.

Chapter 8

'Here you go,' said Jack, holding out three red apples. 'It wouldn't be Halloween without a few apples. You can bob for them later.'

'Apple?' grunted the skeleton.

'Bob?' said the mummy.

'Mine!' said the jack-o'-lantern, snatching an apple from Jack's hand. It held the apple to the jagged line that had been carved for its mouth.

Good luck shoving a whole apple through there, thought Jack.

But then the jack-o'-lantern's mouth miraculously opened wide and took a bite.

And another and another and another.

'Omnomnomnom!'

Jack stared in disbelief.

The jack-o'-lantern swallowed the apple core afterwards with a big gulp.

'What the hell?' said Jack.

Its head couldn't be a real pumpkin, after all. The mouth had opened and closed like living flesh. A mask then? An animatronic mask?

But then things got weird.

The jack-o'-lantern groaned and clutched its stomach. It shuddered violently and its pumpkin-head started to redden. The head swelled outwards and upwards, whilst a stem the size and thickness of a marker pen sprouted from the top.

Jack gaped.

The jack-o'-lantern's pumpkin-head had transformed into an apple-head.

'What – What the – '

The other two trick-or-treaters turned to Jack and hissed at him.

'Trick,' said the skeleton, pointing an accusing bony finger.

'Trick,' repeated the mummy.

'No,' stammered Jack. 'I didn't know it would do that.'

The jack-o'-lantern shuddered again, prompting the reverse to happen. The apple-head reverted into its pumpkin-head through a series of violent jerks, leaving the jack-o'-lantern bent double, gasping.

'Trick,' it spat, pointing at Jack.

'No, please,' said Jack. 'How was I supposed to know you were allergic?'

'Trick! Trick! Trick!'

Jack realised he was dealing with real monsters, not ordinary trick-or-treaters. Halloween was supposedly the time of year when the fabric of the world grew thin and creatures could pass through from the other side. Looking at the three creatures on his doorstep, he could believe it.

Three *angry* creatures.

'I'm sorry,' said Jack, shrinking back. 'Here. Forget the apples. I have other things for you.'

'Sugar!'

'No, I don't have any chocolate left but – '

'No apples!'

'Yes, got it, no more apples. How about this?'

To give the monsters money, turn to page 43.
To give the monsters gum, turn to page 63.

Chapter 9

'Here you go,' said Jack, holding out a packet of gum. 'Chewing gum. Great for stimulating saliva. It will wash away some of that sugar and keep your teeth in good order.'

'Gum?' grunted the jack-o'-lantern.

'Saliva?' said the skeleton.

'Hold out your hands, kids,' said Jack.

Jack dropped a capsule of gum onto each outstretched palm: one bandaged, one skeletal and one gloved. All three stared warily at the gum as though it were an alien entity.

'You'll like it,' promised Jack. 'Minty.'

The mummy tentatively lifted the gum to the mouth-slit in its bandages and chucked it inside. Jack watched the mummy's jaw start to chew.

'See,' said Jack. 'It's important to look after your teeth.'

But then things got strange.

The mummy suddenly went rigid. Its jaundiced eyes opened wide in shock. The sharpness of the mint flavouring must have been too much. A jet of steam burst forth from its mouth, like a kettle coming to the boil, only minty and fragrant. The mummy's bandages ruffled from the shock, like a set of venetian window blinds caught in a gust of wind.

'Kid, are you okay?' asked Jack.

Then the mummy's right arm fell off.

Jack gaped.

'What – What the – '

The other two trick-or-treaters turned to Jack and hissed at him.

'Trick,' said the skeleton, pointing an accusing bony finger.

'Trick,' repeated the jack-o'-lantern.

'No,' stammered Jack, now starting to comprehend what was standing on his doorstep. 'I didn't know that would happen.'

Thankfully, the mummy recovered just as quickly. Its rigid body went slack once again and the steam ceased to issue from its mouth. Only then did the mummy notice its right arm on the floor. It snatched the arm up with its left hand, wedging it back into the shoulder joint with a matter-of-fact twist.

'Trick,' it groaned, pointing at Jack.

'No, please,' said Jack. 'How was I supposed to know you were allergic?'

'Trick! Trick! Trick!'

Jack realised he was dealing with real monsters, not ordinary trick-or-treaters. Halloween was supposedly the time of year when the fabric of the world grew thin and creatures could pass through from the other side. Looking at the three creatures on his doorstep, he could believe it.

Three *angry* creatures.

'I'm sorry,' he said, shrinking back. 'Here. Forget the gum. I have other things for you.'

'Sugar!'

'No, I don't have any chocolate left but – '

'No gum!'

'Yes, got it, no more gum. How about this?'

To give the monsters fruit, turn to page 66.

To give the monsters money, turn to page 69.

Chapter 10

'Or *this*, you little shit.'

Jack lunged forward. He was pleased to see the youth dart backwards, scared by Jack's sudden movement, but Jack wasn't going after the lad. He was going after his sweets. Jack snatched up his Aldi bag and chucked it into the hallway behind him.

'Thanks!' cheered Jack. 'More treats for me!'

'Give those back!' shouted the boy, enraged.

Jack slammed the door in his face. He expected an immediate volley of eggs to splatter against the door but instead he got angry, hammering fists. The lad attacked like an animal, unable to vocalise his threats, such was his fury. Instead, he shouted an incoherent barrage of swearwords.

Jack helped himself to one of the youth's chocolate bars to steel his nerves.

Eventually, *eventually*, the hammering and swearing ceased.

'Right, last chance,' said the boy through the letterbox. 'Give me back my treats.'

'They're my treats now,' said Jack. The sugar high from the chocolate bar had made him reckless. 'Spoils of war.'

'The war has only just begun, mate. I'll be back.'

Jack scoffed, snaffling down a second chocolate bar. 'Off to get more eggs from Aldi? You better hurry. They close at ten.'

'No, mate,' sniggered the leader. 'Off to get reinforcements. My Uncle Finn isn't far away.'

Jack suddenly lost his appetite. His bravery melted in an instant.

'Enjoy my treats whilst you still have teeth,' taunted the lad. 'We'll hit you with more than eggs when we return.'

'Wait, hold on,' croaked Jack, panicking.

'Too late.'

Jack heard rapid footsteps as the youth sped off to get his uncle.

Uh-oh.

Now what?

To hide in the kitchen, turn to page 206.

To hide in the lounge, turn to page 52.

Chapter 11

'Or nothing,' said Jack, patiently. 'But I'd very much like you to stop.'

'Would you now?' scoffed the teenager. 'You should have given me something decent to eat then.'

Jack took another splattering of eggs but he didn't retaliate. Nor did he run.

'I'm sorry you feel that way,' he said. 'Keep throwing eggs if you must.'

'I will.'

Jack bowed his head in resignation, awaiting the next splat.

'Wait,' said the teenager. 'Do you *like* being egged? Are you getting off on this?'

'God, no!' said Jack.

'Then why aren't you pissed off?'

'Because it's not your fault. You've clearly never been taught how to behave. Children can't be blamed for their mistakes.'

'Children?' repeated the teenager. 'I'm thirteen, mate.'

He threw another egg at Jack, a direct hit, but no others followed. The young lad rummaged around in the pockets of his hoody, aimlessly. It looked like his arsenal of eggs had depleted.

Jack wiped yolk off his face. 'I want you to know, I forgive you.'

'I don't give a shit.'

'Do you want to talk about your actions?' asked Jack, thinking it worth a try. 'Is there a reason for your anger?'

'Because you gave me a sodding apple, you patronising prick.'

'I'm just trying to help.'

'You can help by giving me all of your eggs.'

'I don't have any eggs.'

'Bullshit.'

Without warning, the teen darted past Jack into his house.

'Wait!' cried Jack. 'Stop!'

Turn to page 348.

Chapter 12

'Bloody treat-or-treaters!'

The ringing was followed by a loud hammering of such magnitude that Jack thought they were trying to cave his door in.

'Cheeky little – '

'Open up!' demanded a man's deep voice. 'This is the police.'

Uh oh.

'A domestic disturbance has been reported at this address,' said the police officer. Jack realised that Ivy, the elderly spinster next door, must have heard them arguing. *Nosy old bint.*

'We know you're in there,' said another voice, female. *Christ, two police officers.* 'We heard the television. Come on, now. You would do well to answer.'

The male police officer lost patience. He shouted, 'Open up right now or we'll kick the door down.'

Shit, shit.

Jack panicked. His thoughts became a blur. Hide the body, or run away, or dispose of the police officers – too many options, none of them good. No, the priority was answering the door so they didn't kick it in. Maybe he could keep them talking, make sure they stayed on the doorstep. At the very least, he could keep them in the lounge.

'Coming!' He abandoned the chainsaw in the kitchen and sprinted to the front door. 'On my way!'

Jack swung the door open and sure enough, there were two uniformed –

Wait.

'Ted?' said Jack, incredulous.

'Jack?' said Ted. His wife's lover. 'What are you covered in?'

Shit.

Jack had been rushing so much, his panic levels rising, that he had overlooked the bigger picture. He was still drenched in Joan's blood. He had literally been caught red-handed.

'What did you do?' roared Ted, eyes wide. 'What did you do to Joan?'

Jack returned the angry glower. This was the man who had been fucking his wife. At that moment, he didn't care about getting caught. His only regret was leaving the chainsaw in the kitchen. He would love to drive it through Ted's stomach.

But Jack was unarmed and Ted moved first. The police officer drew his baton and struck Jack over the head.

Hard.

Flip a coin.

If heads, turn to page 55.

If tails, turn to page 60.

Chapter 13

Ding dong.

Jack shook his head.

The trick-or-treaters could ring his doorbell all night as far as he was concerned. He still wasn't going to answer the door drenched in his wife's blood.

Sorry kids. We're closed for Halloween. Fill up on sugar someplace else.

Jack started scooping up body parts and individually bagging them in black bin bags. He planned to carry them discreetly to the top of his garden, one by one, and out into the wood behind his house. He would then bury them in different locations. Lots of little holes would be quicker to dig, and less noticeable, than digging one enormous hole for an intact body.

Knock, knock.

Jack cursed. The kids had abandoned the

doorbell and were now knocking instead. Quite loudly too.

They better not leave a dent.

Or sticky chocolate fingerprints. Or eggs. If anyone egged his house then he would run outside with his chainsaw and they would meet Hot Head Jack.

Jack ignored the knocking, assuming they would toddle off, and carried on bagging body parts.

'Why did I make so many?'

The novelty of the chainsaw had made him a little over-zealous. He would run out of bin bags at this rate, then he would have to resort to plastic bags from recent shopping trips. Jack had a fair few bags-for-life too, although they were far too nice to bloody and bury. One of them was canvas, for crying out loud.

Knock, knock.

Jack paused at that one.

'Is someone there?' he called.

It had sounded much closer than the front door. It seemed to come from *inside* the house, perhaps on the lounge door. Rather than investigate, and risk being seen in his blood-splattered glory, Jack froze and listened carefully, hardly daring to breathe.

There was no follow-up knock. No footsteps. No conspiratorial whispering.

'Must have imagined – '

Knock, knock.

That one made him jump. It was the closest-sounding knock yet, on the other side of the kitchen door. If the door opened then he would be caught *very* red-handed. Jack leapt at the door, throwing his full weight against it, pressing it shut.

'I don't know who you are,' said Jack. 'But whoever you are, you need to leave. You are trespassing on my property. That is a criminal offense.'

But there was no answer. Had they gone?

Knock, knock! Jack yelped. It had come from the kitchen closet. *Knock, knock!* He jumped again. That one had come from the cupboard under the sink. *Knock, knock!*

'What the hell is happening?'

The third knock had come from the inside of the dishwasher.

'Come in then!' screamed Jack, raising the chainsaw. 'Don't be shy!'

The three doors all slammed open – closet, cupboard, dishwasher – and a trick-or-treater emerged from each one. A skeleton, a jack-o'-lantern and a mummy. Jack whirled around. The trick-or-treaters were on all sides. Something about their masks, their aura, the manner of their appearance, told Jack that these weren't kids in costumes. These were real demons. He recalled that Halloween was supposedly the time of year when the fabric of the world grew thin and creatures could pass through from the other side.

'Trick or treat?' said the skeleton.

'How did you get in here?' asked Jack.

'We can knock on any door, as long as there are tricks and treats inside.' The skeleton sniffed, which was ludicrous considering it lacked a nose. 'And there is an especially nice treat in here.'

'Will you go if I fetch you a bowl of chocolate?' tried Jack, hopefully.

'No, not sugar. You are the treat!'

'Me?'

'Your soul is black with grime. That makes for delicious eating, even sweeter than sugar.'

'You better stay back, all three of you. Or I'll show you a trick.'

Jack pulled the cord of the chainsaw. It sprang into life. He thrust it at the monsters, whirling around to make sure all three were staying back. The trio simply laughed.

'Here's ours,' said the skeleton, clicking its fingers.

The various limbs of Joan's body started gravitating towards each other, rising up, and reassembling to form Joan once again. Only, it wasn't quite Joan. The body parts dangled loosely from each other, not connected by sinew or even string, but rather hanging together by dark magic. Her head lolled from side to side, as did her arms and legs, like a grotesque marionette doll.

She wasn't a zombie. Just a puppet.

Even so –

When the skeleton flicked its wrist, and the Joan puppet flew towards Jack, he was ready with his buzzing chainsaw. He swiped the weapon at Joan, once, twice, missing entirely. The skeleton taunted Jack, moving the puppet towards him, then away again, over and over. The monsters laughed. It was a ghastly chorus: the cackle of the skeleton, the high titter of the jack-o'-lantern, and the low guffaw of the mummy.

Jack was tired of being the fool. His wife and Ted had made a cuckold of him for months, laughing behind his back. Now he was being mocked by demons.

No more.

He ran forward, wielding his chainsaw, with the intention of cutting the Joan puppet apart, then going to town on each and every monster in his kitchen, starting with that fucking skeleton.

But Jack moved too quickly. His feet skidded on the slick, bloodied floor. He slipped backwards, his legs flying out from under him. The buzzing chainsaw flew from his hands, soaring upwards.

Banging the back of his head on the kitchen tiles knocked some sense into him. As he watched the chainsaw reach the zenith of its flight, he paused to think. Had any of it been real? The knocking, the monsters, the Joan puppet? Had the messages on Joan's phone been real, or had he imagined those too? Had he killed his wife over nothing but his own paranoid delusions?

It was an unsettling thought.

The chainsaw raced down towards him –

At least he didn't have to think about it for long.

THE END

Chapter 14

'Money!' said Jack, in a high-pitched voice. He grabbed the piggy bank kept by the front door, into which he and Joan emptied their loose change upon arriving home each day. Jack was now rapidly emptying the change into his hand. 'Money is better than food. You can take it to the shop and buy whatever you want. Chocolate, sweets, crisps, fizzy pop, magazines, toys, anything!'

'Crisps?' grunted the mummy.

'Pop?' said the skeleton.

'Hold out your hands again,' said Jack. 'Both hands. Cup them together.'

The three monsters did hold out their hands – bandaged, skeletal and gloved – though with more suspicion this time. Jack tipped a load of coins into each pair. He exhausted the entire piggy bank. There were some ten and twenty pence coins in the mix. Not a bad haul.

'There's a shop at the bottom of this cul-de-sac,' explained Jack. 'It should still be open. Why don't you go there now?' Then in a louder, pleading, panicky voice, 'Go there now! Go there now!'

The monsters appeared confused by the coins. The jack-o'-lantern sniffed them. The mummy lifted them to the side of its head like a conch shell, apparently expecting them to make a noise. The skeleton considered its coins thoughtfully, tilting its head to one side then the other.

'Have you not seen money before?' asked Jack.

The skeleton responded by scooping the coins into its mouth and throwing its head back, swallowing them in one go.

'I guess not,' said Jack, unblinking. 'They're not – They're not for eating!'

Then things got weird again.

The skeleton jerked painfully as the calcium-white of its bones transformed into silver-bronze metal. Within moments, it fell still, frozen in place.

The jack-o'-lantern and mummy inspected their colleague, now a gleaming metallic statue standing between them. The jack-o'-lantern gave the skeleton's head an experiment rap with its knuckles. The mummy waved a bandaged hand in front of the skeleton's eyeless sockets. Neither action prompted their fellow monster to move.

'Trick!' moaned the mummy.

'Trick!' hissed the jack-o'-lantern.

'It's not my fault!' cried Jack. 'Your mate wasn't supposed to eat the money.'

The jack-o'-lantern took a menacing step forward, the fire within its head glowing extra brightly. The mummy advanced too, loosening a bandage and holding it taut between both hands, intending to strangle Jack.

Thankfully, the effect on the skeleton didn't last much longer. The statuesque figure jerked and the metal receded from its bones, leaving only white once again.

'Trick,' shouted the skeleton, pointing a bony finger at Jack. The tip of the finger was filed into a sharp point.

Strike two, thought Jack.

Fruit, money – What else did he have?

Give the monsters gum, turn to page 73.

Give the monsters a weight loss bar, turn to page 76.

Chapter 15

Virgil checked in with his prize Shark.

'Anything overnight?' he asked.

'Quite a big something,' she said. 'I sent you an email.'

'I've not looked at my inbox. Busy night.'

'How busy?'

Virgil raised his takeaway coffee cup. 'This is a quadruple espresso. No joke.'

'You really should make the move to matcha.'

'Not the morning after Halloween.'

'And get a reusable cup. You save 25p each time.'

'So you keep telling me.'

'And you save the planet.'

'I already save the planet. Daily.'

The Shark was undeterred. 'I'll buy you a reusable cup.' She paused. '*If* I get you for Secret Santa this year.'

Virgil yawned. 'You mentioned a big something?'

'That's right.'

'Whereabouts? This country?'

'The Midlands. A place called Sutton Coldfield.'

Virgil blinked. 'Satan Coldfield?'

'No, *Sutton* Coldfield. Although Satan might be a more fitting name.'

'How do you mean?'

'There was a reality breach. A few actually.'

'Go on.'

'A trio of demons showed up on some poor bloke's doorstep.'

'They did?'

'Trick or treating.'

'You're kidding.'

'My nose is never wrong. It escalated pretty quickly. They invaded his home.'

'Poor bloke, indeed.'

'Don't worry, he had help.'

'Not from us. We were stretched too thinly last night. Bloody austerity.'

'He had help from a saint.'

'Helpful neighbor?'

'No, an actual saint.'

'What, like, from Heaven?'

'Yep. Eustace Hubertus, the patron saint of hunting.'

Virgil pinched the bridge of his nose. 'Okay,' he said slowly.

'The saint did his best, but the three demons morphed into Balam, a Duke of Hell. It looked pretty bad for a while, but the human was smart. He kept the Duke talking until midnight.'

'What happens at midnight? Do demons turn back into pumpkins?'

'No, clever clogs. Halloween ends and All Saint's Day begins.'

'This coffee hasn't kicked in yet. You need to spell it out.'

'Demons lose their power and saints gain a boost.'

'Meaning?'

'A load more saints rocked up and defeated the demon.'

'The good guys won?'

'That's right.'

Virgil winced. 'So we have a surviving witness.'

'And he witnessed a *lot* of weird stuff. You might want to pay him a visit.'

'You heard me say we're stretched, right?'

'Yes, boss. Your call.'

Virgil scratched his head. 'That is a lot of reality breaches in one spot.'

'I did some sniffing around.' Virgil knew the Shark meant literally. 'The fabric is very thin around there. A few rips in places.'

Virgil cursed. 'Then why haven't we noticed more incidents until now?'

'Two possible reasons, the way I see it.' The Shark stretched back into her beanbag. 'Firstly, the fabric breaches are new. Something happened to rock the boat in this Sutton Coldfield place.'

'Or secondly?'

'The thinness has always been there.' The Shark grinned. 'You've only had my nose in your employ for a few months. No other Sharks come close to my ability. You said so yourself.'

'And it's gone to your head, I see.'

'Your words.' The Shark sipped her matcha.

'Okay then,' said Virgil. 'Keep an eye – a nose –

on Satan Coldfield.'

'*Sutton* Coldfield.'

'That too.' He frowned. 'Sutton Coldfield. Why does that ring a bell?'

'I emailed you about it, remember?'

'Never mind. It'll come to me. Just monitor the place carefully.'

'No problem, boss. My nose is at your service. What are you going to do?'

Virgil had no idea.

'I'm going to get another coffee.'

TO BE CONTINUED

Chapter 16

Jack felt weak at the knees. He needed to sit down. He staggered into the lounge and collapsed onto the sofa.

'Now what do I do?'

Naturally, he did what every human being did in a crisis: he pulled out his phone. Though, after staring at the screen in careful consideration, he quickly pocketed it again.

'No,' he said to himself. 'No police.'

There were two reasons why Jack couldn't call the police.

Firstly, Joan was a police officer. She was on duty right now. He had dropped her off earlier in the evening for her shift. If a call came through the radio about an incident at her *own* address then her police car would arrive within minutes. If the youth really did intend to return with a violent uncle then that would put Joan in harm's way. Admittedly, Joan put herself at risk every time she wore her uniform, but this was a dangerous situation of Jack's own devising. Anything bad that happened as a result would be his fault. What if this Uncle Finn bloke pulled a knife on her?

Secondly, Joan was a police officer. What if there was no Uncle Finn? What if Jack called the police because he had gotten himself hoodwinked by a twelve-year old trick-or-treater? That sort of thing spread around the force like wildfire. Jack would be a laughing stock to all of Joan's colleagues, plus they would never let Joan live it down either.

'No police,' he repeated.

Jack's temper had gotten him into this mess, so it was his responsibility, and his alone, to defend the house against any intruders. Even so: easier said than done.

He considered his phone again. There must be a YouTube tutorial on how to defend your home against attackers. There was a YouTube tutorial for everything, right? But did he have time to watch a film on his phone?

Films. That was it.

Jack didn't need to watch a YouTube tutorial for inspiration. He had been watching films all of his life. Better yet, his and Joan's favourite films had given him all the pointers he would ever need to defend his home. He turned to the DVD cabinet to steel his nerves.

To choose Joan's favourite film, turn to page 88.

To choose Jack's favourite film, turn to page 93.

Chapter 17

Jack awoke slowly, his head throbbing.

He was handcuffed to a chair in the lounge. One of the kitchen chairs, it seemed, with the straight wooden back. The police officers had been in the kitchen.

Bugger.

It explained Ted's angry pacing. He stomped back and forth, breathing heavily, clenching and unclenching his fists. The police officer seemed unable to decide whether to howl with grief or rage after discovering his lover dismembered on the kitchen floor. Jack could smell vomit, so he guessed Ted had already emptied his stomach with disgust.

Great. Something else to clean up. If I ever get out of this chair.

Jack watched the pacing unfold through squinted eyes. He didn't want to open them fully, partly because the light was too bright for his sore head, but mostly because he wanted to eavesdrop.

'Ted, we have to call this in,' said the female police officer. She looked uneasy but was clearly made of stronger stuff than her partner. At least she could stand still and formulate words. 'Ted, listen to me.'

Jack vaguely recalled meeting her at one of Joan's Christmas parties. Each year, they hosted a festive soirée which brought together every police officer and their spouse. What was her name? Sarah, Susan, Sienna –

'No, Sophie,' said Ted.

Almost had it.

Ted pointed at Jack. 'This scumbag deserves worse than prison,' said Ted, pointing a damning finger at Jack. 'He cut up his wife, for crying out loud.'

'And he'll go down for life,' said Sophie. 'An immediate conviction. The evidence is overwhelming.'

'No, no, no,' said Ted, shaking his head. 'That's not how it works these days. He'll cry mental health. Say he wasn't acting of rational mind. Before you know it, he'll be getting mollycoddled in a mental health facility, most likely end up with a reduced sentence for good behaviour.'

'That's not for us to decide.'

'Not normally, but tonight, I'm the judge. I sentence him to a night of pain. I want him to feel the same fear and agony that Joan must have felt.'

'You mustn't.'

'That's Joan in there, you know,' snapped Ted, squaring up to his colleague. Sophie was surprisingly unnerved by the larger, wild-eyed man.

'I know,' she said steadily.

'Our fellow police officer. Our friend.'

'And your lover.'

Ted hesitated. 'I'm sorry?'

'We all know about you and Joan. You were terrible at hiding it.'

'You did?' Ted let himself get distracted by that revelation. 'But we were so careful. Only ever met in hotels. I didn't even know where she lived.'

'Didn't stop you both snogging in the locker room.'

'Well, whatever.' He threw up his hands. 'It's over

now, thanks to this evil fucker.'

Jack thought it was time to wake up. 'Do your worst, Ted.' He was pleased to see Ted jump at the sound of his voice.

'Oh, I will,' said Ted, snatching up his baton from the television cabinet where it had been lying. He gripped it so tightly that his knuckles turned white.

Jack figured if he was going to be tortured by his wife's lover then he might as well torture the twat in return. 'Ted, you should know, Joan suffered a *lot*. It'll take some doing to make me hurt the same as she did in her final moments.'

'Shut your mouth!'

'This is all your fault, Ted,' said Jack with a smarmy grin. 'I loved my wife until you tempted her away. She'd still be alive if it wasn't for you.'

'I said shut your mouth!'

'It's all on you, Ted. All on you.'

Ted let out a furious shriek and raised his baton high above his head. It would be a devastating blow but Jack was ready. Better to die here, quickly, tormenting his wife's lover, then spend a lifetime in prison.

Bring it on.

If you are reading this at home, turn to page 95.

If you are reading this elsewhere, turn to page 99.

Chapter 18

Jack awoke, courtesy of a slap to the face.

'Wake up, you piece of shit,' said a voice. Ted's voice. 'I want you to be awake for this.'

Jack waded up into consciousness, his head hurting like hell, and now his cheek stinging too. He discovered that he was handcuffed to a chair in the lounge. A kitchen chair. Ah. That meant they had been into the kitchen and seen his handiwork, seen Joan's body scattered like a jigsaw freshly-poured from the box.

Not good.

Ted was holding the murder weapon in his hand, the enormous kitchen knife. Something about the way he held the knife made Jack think he didn't want to bag the blade for evidence. There was a mad glint in his eye.

Also not good.

'You butchered her, you fuck,' shouted Ted.

Jack might have been more panicked but there was still hope. The second police officer, the woman, the one he had heard through the door, stood watching the scene unfold. It was Sophie, another of Joan's colleagues who he knew well from various Christmas parties. He had a special bond with Sophie. She would stop Ted from doing anything rash.

'Ted, put the knife down,' she said. 'We need to call this in. You don't want to get arrested yourself.'

'Come on, Sophie, who would know?'

'I would.'

'Prison is too good for this monster. I loved Joan, I loved her.'

'Yes, we all know about your affair.'

'Good for you. We weren't hiding it from the team, just this evil fucker here. I didn't even know where she lived. We stuck to hotels.'

'Evil fucker' was one insult too many from his wife's lover and the reference to hotels did nothing to improve Jack's temper. Time to stick in a knife of his own. Figuratively.

'Joan's death is on you, Ted,' he announced. 'I

never would have killed her if you hadn't tempted her away from me.'

'Don't you dare say that,' said Ted, pointing the knife at him.

'This is your fault. Her blood is on your hands.'

'Stop talking.'

'So thanks Ted. I hope you are proud of yourself.'

'Shut up!'

'You ruined our marriage and ruined our lives.'

'I said shut up!'

'And Joan lost hers because of you.'

'No!'

Jack had hoped the taunting would reduce Ted to a blubbering mess, or at least give Sophie time to disarm him. It even seemed to be working for a while.

Instead, Ted snapped and drove the kitchen knife down into Jack's thigh.

'Aaaarrr – !'

If your year of birth is an even year, turn to page 102.
If your year of birth is an odd year, turn to page 105.

Chapter 19

'Here you go!' said Jack, in a panicky voice. He held out a packet of gum. 'Chewing gum. Great for stimulating saliva. It will help wash away some of that sugar and keep your teeth in good order.'

'Gum?' grunted the jack-o'-lantern.

'Saliva?' said the skeleton.

'Hold out your hands,' said Jack.

The three monsters did just that. Jack dropped a capsule of gum onto each palm: one gloved, one skeletal, and one bandaged. All three stared warily at the gum as though it were an alien concept to them.

'You'll like it,' promised Jack. 'Minty.'

The mummy tentatively lifted the gum to its mouth-slit and chucked it inside. Jack watched the mummy's jaw start to masticate.

'See,' said Jack. 'It's important to look after your teeth.'

But then things got strange.

The mummy went rigid, its jaundiced eyes opening wide in shock. The sharpness of the mint flavouring must have been too much. A jet of steam burst forth from its mouth, like a kettle coming to the boil, only minty and fragrant. The mummy's bandages ruffled from the shock, like a set of venetian window blinds caught in a gust.

'Erm, are you okay?' asked Jack.

The mummy's right arm fell off.

Jack gaped.

'What – What the – '

The other two trick-or-treaters turned to Jack and hissed at him.

'Trick,' said the skeleton, pointing an accusing bony finger.

'Trick,' repeated the jack-o'-lantern.

'No,' stammered Jack. 'I didn't know it would do that.'

Thankfully, the mummy recovered. Its rigid body went slack once again. The steam ceased to issue from its mouth. Only then did the mummy notice its right arm on the floor. It snatched the arm up with its left hand and wedged it back into the shoulder joint with a matter-of-fact twist.

'Trick,' it groaned, pointing at Jack.

'No, please,' said Jack. 'I didn't know.'

'Trick! Trick! Trick!'

Strike two, thought Jack.

Fruit, gum – What else did he have?

Give the monsters money, turn to page 110.

Give the monsters a weight loss bar, turn to page 76.

Chapter 20

'Here you go!' said Jack, in a high-pitched voice. He held out three red apples. 'It wouldn't be Halloween without a few apples. You can bob for them later.'

'Apple?' grunted the skeleton.

'Bob?' said the mummy.

'Mine!' said the jack-o'-lantern, snatching an apple from Jack's hand. It held the apple to the jagged line that had been carved for its mouth.

Good luck shoving a whole apple through there, thought Jack.

But then the jack-o'-lantern's mouth miraculously opened wide and took a bite from the apple. And another and another and another.

'Omnomnomnom!'

Jack stared in disbelief.

The pumpkin swallowed the apple core afterwards with a big gulp.

'What the hell?' said Jack.

It couldn't be a real pumpkin, after all. The mouth had opened and closed like living flesh. A mask then? An animatronic mask?

But then things got weird.

The jack-o'-lantern groaned and clutched its stomach. It shuddered violently and its pumpkin-head started to redden, swell outwards and upwards, whilst a stem the size and thickness of a marker pen sprouted from the top of its head.

Jack gaped.

The jack-o'-lantern's pumpkin-head had transformed into an apple-head.

'What – What the – '

The other two trick-or-treaters turned to Jack and hissed at him.

'Trick,' said the skeleton, pointing an accusing bony finger.

'Trick,' repeated the mummy.

'No,' stammered Jack. 'I'm not doing this on purpose.'

The jack-o'-lantern shuddered again, prompting the reverse to happen. The apple-head reformed into its pumpkin-head through a series of violent jerks, leaving the jack-o'-lantern bent double, gasping.

'Trick,' it spat, pointing at Jack.

'No, please,' said Jack. 'I didn't know.'

'Trick! Trick! Trick!'

'I'm sorry,' he said, shrinking back.

Strike two, thought Jack.

Gum, fruit – What else did he have?

Give the monsters money, turn to page 117.

Give the monsters a weight loss bar, turn to page 76.

Chapter 21

'Money!' said Jack, in a high-pitched voice. He grabbed the piggy bank kept by the front door, into which he and Joan emptied their loose change upon arriving home each day. Jack was now rapidly emptying the change into his hand. 'Money is better than food. You can take it to the shop and buy whatever you want. Chocolate, sweets, crisps, fizzy pop, magazines, toys, anything!'

'Crisps?' grunted the mummy.

'Pop?' said the skeleton.

'Hold out your hands again,' said Jack. 'Both hands. Cup them together.'

The three monsters did hold out their hands – bandaged, skeletal and gloved – though with more suspicion this time. Jack tipped a load of coins into each pair. He exhausted the entire piggy bank. There were some ten and twenty pence coins in the mix. Not a bad haul.

'There's a shop at the bottom of this cul-de-sac,' explained Jack. 'It should still be open. Why don't you go there now?' Then in a louder, pleading, panicky voice, 'Go there now! Go there now!'

The monsters appeared confused by the coins. The jack-o'-lantern sniffed them. The mummy lifted them to the side of its head like a conch shell, apparently expecting them to make a noise. The skeleton considered its coins thoughtfully, tilting its head to one side then the other.

'Have you not seen money before?' asked Jack.

The skeleton responded by scooping the coins into its mouth and throwing its head back, swallowing them in one go.

'I guess not,' said Jack, unblinking. 'They're not – They're not for eating!'

Then things got weird again.

The skeleton jerked painfully as the calcium-white of its bones transformed into silver-bronze metal. Within moments, it fell still, frozen in place.

The jack-o'-lantern and mummy inspected their colleague, now a gleaming metallic statue. The jack-o'-lantern gave the skeleton's head an experiment rap with its knuckles. The mummy waved a bandaged hand in front of the skeleton's eyeless sockets. Neither action prompted their fellow monster to move.

'Trick!' moaned the mummy.

'Trick!' hissed the jack-o'-lantern.

'It's not my fault!' cried Jack. 'Your mate wasn't supposed to eat the money.'

The jack-o'-lantern took a menacing step forward, the fire within its head glowing extra brightly. The mummy advanced too, loosening a bandage and holding it taut between both hands, intending to strangle Jack.

Thankfully, the effect on the skeleton didn't last much longer. The statuesque figure jerked and the metal receded from its bones, leaving only white once again.

'Trick,' shouted the skeleton, pointing a bony finger at Jack. The tip of the finger was filed into a sharp point.

Strike two, thought Jack.

Gum, money – What else did he have?

Give the monsters fruit, turn to page 114.

Give the monsters a weight loss bar, turn to page 76.

Chapter 22

'Here you go!' said Jack, voice flooded with desperation. 'Chewing gum. Great for stimulating saliva. It will help wash away some of that sugar and keep your teeth in good order.'

'Gum?' grunted the jack-o'-lantern.

'Saliva?' said the skeleton.

'Hold out your hands, kids,' said Jack.

Jack dropped a capsule of gum onto each palm: one bandaged, one skeletal and one gloved. All three stared warily at the gum as though it were an alien entity.

'You'll like it,' promised Jack. 'Minty.'

The mummy tentatively lifted the gum to the mouth-slit in its bandages and chucked it inside. Jack watched the mummy's jaw start to chew.

'See,' said Jack. 'It's important to look after your teeth.'

But then things got strange.

The mummy suddenly went rigid. Its jaundiced eyes opened wide in shock. The sharpness of the mint flavouring must have been too much. A jet of steam burst forth from its mouth, like a kettle coming to the boil, only minty and fragrant. The mummy's bandages ruffled from the shock, like a set of venetian window blinds caught in a gust of wind.

'Kid, are you okay?' asked Jack.

Then the mummy's right arm fell off.

Jack gaped.

'What – What the – '

The other two trick-or-treaters turned to Jack and hissed at him.

'Trick,' said the skeleton, pointing an accusing bony finger.

'Trick,' repeated the jack-o'-lantern.

'No,' stammered Jack, now starting to comprehend what was standing on his doorstep. 'I didn't know that would happen.'

Thankfully, the mummy recovered. Its rigid body went slack once again and the steam ceased to issue from its mouth. Only then did the mummy notice its right arm on the floor. It snatched the arm up with its left hand, wedging it back in at the shoulder joint with a matter-of-fact twist.

'Trick,' it groaned, pointing at Jack.

'No, please,' said Jack. 'I'm not doing this on purpose!'

'Trick! Trick! Trick!'

'Wait, wait,' he pleaded. 'Give me another chance.'

Strike three, thought Jack.

Fruit, money, gum –

He only had one option left.

Give the monsters a weight loss bar, turn to page 76.

To explain the situation, turn to page 129.

Chapter 23

'I know, I know!' cried Jack, hysterically. 'Wait here!'

He sprinted through the house as though his life depended on it – which it probably did – and returned to the front door with a box of Joan's weight loss bars.

'Cereal bars,' he panted. 'One each.'

Joan didn't need to lose weight, never had, yet she brought a box every week all the same. Thank God she did. He doubly thanked God that there were exactly three bars inside.

Jack offered the first bar to the skeleton. He thought of the skeleton as the leader, partly because it stood in the middle, but mostly because it wore that jaunty top hat.

'Trick?' said the skeleton, eyeing the bar cautiously, not that it *had* eyeballs.

'Not a trick, I promise,' said Jack. 'Food. Healthy

food. Hardly any calories.'

'Sugar?' it asked.

Not quite, thought Jack. *Completely sugar free and they taste pretty damn awful too.*

But at least he was offering them food. Supposedly, the bars contained natural sweeteners, though they tasted like sawdust in Jack's opinion.

'Tasty,' lied Jack. He held the bar to his mouth and mimed biting it, then rubbed a hand over his tummy in a circular motion. 'Hmmmm! Yummy, and a great way to lose –' He considered the fleshless skeleton. 'Never mind.'

The three monsters stared distrustfully, so Jack tore open the wrapper of his bar and bit off a tiny corner.

Blurgh. Yuk. Blah.

Flavourless, dry, stale. Jack could feel himself losing weight just by eating it because it sure as hell wasn't filling him up.

Speaking of Hell –

The three monsters finally accepted that food was being offered, each snatching a bar from Jack. They ripped off the wrappers simultaneously and wolfed them down in feral bites. Next, they waited, anticipating a side effect, another trick.

Jack half-expected one himself. He waited for them to mutate into cereal mannequins before his very eyes. If they did, that would be one strike too many and he wouldn't get another chance to save himself from their retaliation. He doubted a slammed door would slow down three creatures from Satan's inner circle.

Thankfully, the monsters appeared to be fine, though they weren't happy.

'Blurgh!'

'Yuk!'

'Blah!'

They growled and groaned and spat, shaking their heads in disgust. The skeleton desperately tried to unpick bits of cereal from its teeth.

'Not a fan?' said Jack, weakly. 'Those are the only other thing I had.'

Turn to page 222.

Chapter 24

The year was 2019.

Most houses had a smart speaker in Jack and Joan's neighbourhood.

'Alexa,' said Jack. 'I need your help.'

The cylindrical speaker awoke with its signature corona of blue light.

'Sure. How can I help?'

'Alexa – '

There was a loud thudding noise. Uncle Finn was booting his front door.

'Are you kidding me?'

'I'm very serious, except when I'm telling jokes. Why do vampires read The Telegraph?'

'No Alexa, no jokes, I want you to – '

Jack heard the front door crash open.

'Fuck.'

'Sorry, I'm not that kind of girl.'

'Alexa – '

He heard the lounge door slam open. The intruders were one room away.

'Where are you?' bellowed Uncle Finn.

'I'm right here.'

'No, Alexa – '

A huge man burst into the kitchen. The trick-or-treating youth skittered in behind his uncle, excited by the promise of violence. Uncle Finn pointed at Jack. 'You're dead.'

'I'm not really alive, but I can be lively sometimes.'

Jack retreated, putting the kitchen island in between himself and Uncle Finn.

'Alexa, call the police!' Jack finally completed his command.

'Who the fuck is Alexa?' shouted Uncle Finn.

'Dialing.'

'Who said that?'

Jack smiled. Most houses had a smart speaker, but not every house it would seem.

'Hello, emergency services,' said a new voice coming from the smart speaker. *'What service do you require?'*

'Police!' shouted Jack. Then very quickly, 'There's

a man in my house, six foot, broken nose, tattoo on the right side of his neck – '

'Oh shit, Uncle Finn,' cried the youth. 'This fucker called the police.'

'Cars are being deployed,' said the voice.

'Good for him,' grunted Uncle Finn. 'They won't get here in time.'

Uncle Finn darted around the island. He moved quicker than Jack had expected for such a big man and grabbed him by the scruff of his jumper.

'But they have your description,' whined the boy.

'Lots of blokes around here have a broken nose,' said Uncle Finn, pulling back a ring-lined fist, intended for Jack's face.

'But only one bloke with your voice,' said Jack, wincing. 'Alexa has a recording of your voice, all stored safely on the Cloud.'

'You fucking what?'

'The police have it too. Voice recognition is more damning than a fingerprint nowadays.'

'Oh, shit.' The penny dropped quicker for the young lad. 'Uncle Finn, we've got to go.'

The boy sped out of the kitchen. Uncle Finn,

clearly confused, thought it safer to follow his nephew, more troubled by the youth's alarm than Jack's words.

But not before growling at Jack, 'We're taking back our sweets.'

Jack almost laughed. As parting blows went, it wasn't the strongest –

Uncle Finn drove his fist into Jack's face.

Now *that* was a strong parting blow.

Turn to page 351.

Chapter 25

The year was 2039.

Every house had a smart speaker. Jack and Joan had one in every room.

'Alexa,' said Jack. 'I need your help.'

The cylindrical speaker awoke with its signature corona of blue light.

'Sure. How can I help?'

'Phone the police.'

There was a loud thudding noise. Somebody was booting his front door. Uncle Finn, presumably.

'I'm sorry. I don't know that one.'

Jack groaned. 'Damn it, Joan.'

Joan had expressly forbid Jack from enabling the Telephone Skill, which would have allowed him to pair his phone with Alexa. She said it gave the machine too much power. Nor was he allowed to pair his bank account or Outlook calendar. Joan had apparently read about a smart speaker in New Europe which had blackmailed its owners. Another in the Republic of Scotland had taken its owners hostage. It all sounded like tabloid nonsense to Jack –

He heard his front door crash open.

'Where are you?' bellowed Uncle Finn.

Luckily, Alexa had other tricks up her sleeve.

'Alexa, kill the lights.'

'Turning off lights.'

The house plunged into darkness. Jack crouched behind the kitchen island and listened carefully. He could hear voices, now in the lounge. The trick-or-treating lad whined, 'Uncle Finn, I don't like the dark.'

'Grow up, Kurt,' snapped the older man. 'Alexa, turn on the lights.'

But Alexa would only respond to Jack or Joan.

'Fuck you then,' said Uncle Finn. 'Luckily I brought my own light.'

Schvrmmmmmmm.

'Oh Christ.' Jack thought he recognised that sound. He whispered, 'Alexa, show me the intruders.'

Jack and Joan had extensions of the smart

speaker in every room. Each had a built-in camera –
a standard feature of the newer models.

'*Here.*'

Alexa projected a hologram onto the kitchen
counter, transmitting what her lounge counterpart
was seeing. It showed Uncle Finn and his nephew in
the lounge. The former was wielding a light dagger.
Some genius had invented them ten years ago, based
on the lightsabre from the Star Wars saga. The
schematics were leaked online and suddenly light
daggers were popping up everywhere. The wrong
person asking the right questions could secure a
cheap knock-off on the Dark Web for a price.

'Show yourself mate,' demanded Uncle Finn. 'I
want to introduce you to my friend here.'

Schvrmmmmmmm. Schvrmmmmmmm.

Even the cheap models could lop off an arm in
one swipe.

Think Jack, he told himself. *What else can Alexa
do?*

He had an idea.

Jack balled up two tea towels and held them
tightly over his ears. He felt bad for Ivy next door,

but she was half-deaf anyway, right? If she wasn't, then she would be after this –

'Alexa,' said Jack, heart pounding. 'Play thrash metal. All speakers. Turn it up to eleven.'

'Playing thrash metal playlist on Spotify.'

The house erupted with traumatic, deafening noise. The hologram showed the two intruders in the lounge slap their hands over their ears. Uncle Finn had moved his hands so quickly that he almost drove his light dagger into his own skull. That would have ended the intrusion nice and quickly.

Something else in the hologram caught Jack's eye, stationed right next to the intruders.

'Alexa,' he shouted over the din. 'Bleed the radiator in the lounge.'

'Bleeding the radiator.'

Jack knew the radiator was red-hot. Joan seemed to think that October was mid-Winter in the Arctic Circle, so the bleeding prompted the radiator to blast out a jet of hissing, burning steam.

'Argh!' roared Uncle Finn.

'Fuck this!' The boy gave up, sprinting for the front door. His uncle charged in the other direction, leaving the scene depicted in the hologram, and heading towards –

The kitchen door flung open. Uncle Finn barged in, scorched and wet and gasping. His glaring eyes found Jack. The intruder raised his light dagger.

Jack's only chance now was negotiation.

'Alexa, stop the music,' said Jack. Blissful silence returned. His lowered the balled-up tea towels from his ears, very aware of the Princess Leia association. 'Now, listen, Mr Finn – '

But Uncle Finn marched forward. 'Let's see if you can still call for Alexa after I slice off your tongue.'

So much for negotiation.

Turn to page 352.

Chapter 26

Finn huffed.

He wasn't a fan of his troublesome nephew, but he couldn't let people disrespect his family. He was Clarence "Fingers" Finnegan for fuck's sake. He had a reputation to uphold.

'This is the place, Uncle Finn,' said Kurt.

'Anyone else at home?'

'Don't know. Think he's home alone.'

'Right, then. Let's have a word.' Finn hammered on the door with his fist. The gold signet rings lining his fingers amplified the sound. 'Open up, mate, or I'll kick this door down.'

No response, of course. The posh prick inside was probably shitting himself. Not good enough. He tried the door handle –

'Ow, fuck!'

'What is it, Uncle Finn?'

'This bastard door knob is red-hot.'

'Hot?'

'The prick must have done something to it.'

Finn growled and booted the door with practised aim. It wasn't Finn's first booting and the door burst open easily. He stepped into the hallway, followed by his drivelling nephew. As Finn suspected, the bloke who lived here had hung an electric charcoal starter over the inside of the door handle, like a Do Not Disturb sign in a hotel. The heat conducted through the metal to the outside handle.

'Where are you, mate?' bellowed Finn, his hand still smarting. 'This is your last chance for a mild beating.'

He stormed into the lounge –

'Ugh!'

Finn walked face-first into a large sheet of sticky cling film, suspended at head-height on the other side of the door. He peeled it off with two hands. 'Son of a bitch.'

'What is it?' asked Kurt.

'What does it look like, you idiot?' he snapped. 'Glue!'

'Why would he want to glue your face?'

'Because he's a dead man.'

Finn stormed into the kitchen. The door was ajar. Only upon entering did he realise *why* the door was ajar. A bag of feathers sat poised on top of the door and tumbled over Finn as he entered. The feathers stuck to his glued-up face. He spat out a mouthful of feathers and roared with rage.

'Hah!' His nephew clearly had no regard for self-preservation because he pointed and laughed.

Finn fumed and cuffed Kurt over the head. 'You better stop that right now, you little shit. I'm only here because you're too useless to deal with your own problems.'

Kurt shut up, as well he should. Finn had always made damn sure his nephew was afraid of him. A few slaps from time to time did the kid some good. He needed toughening up. He was a Finnegan, after all.

'Where are you, dead man?' shouted Finn, addressing the house. He strode into the kitchen. There were lots of places in a kitchen where a posh prick could hide. More than that, Finn needed some ice for his burnt hand.

As it turned out, he found more ice than he

bargained for.

'Whoa!'

Finn's legs flew out from under him. The prick had covered his kitchen floor in tray after tray of ice cubes. At least Finn landed on his nephew, which worked wonders in stopping him from laughing his insufferable head off like a moron.

Finn cautiously rose to his feet, mindful of the ice, and bellowed, 'I'm going to rip your head off!'

'Uncle Finn,' whined Kurt. 'I landed funny.'

'Get up, right now!' He yanked his nephew up by the scruff of his hoody. 'Stop whining. You dragged me into this mess, so man up and take some responsibility. You're a Finnegan, not a chicken shit.'

'You're the chicken, Uncle Finn,' said Kurt, pointing at Finn's feather-covered face. Finn might have been proud of his nephew for that comeback had Finn not already been the victim of three booby traps. He raised his hand, fully-intending to backhand some manners into the boy but –

'I'm up here, you jerks,' called a voice from upstairs.

'You are a dead man!' shouted Finn. To his

nephew, he said, 'After you.'

'What?'

'You're going first, if you think you're so brave.'

'But – '

Finn shoved Kurt, and kept shoving him, until they reached the bottom of the stairs.

'Up you go,' said Finn.

Turn to page 356.

Chapter 27

'This is the place, Uncle Finn,' said Kurt.

'Are you sure?' replied Finn. His nephew wasn't the most reliable source of information. All lights were off except for the flickering candle of the pumpkin in the window.

'Yeah, definitely. He must be hiding inside.'

'Not for long. Let's get your bag of treats back.' He massaged the gold signet rings which lined his fingers. 'Teach this posh prick some manners whilst we're at it.'

Kurt's eyes lit up with excitement. 'Are you going to kick the door in?'

'What do you think?'

Finn booted the door with well-practised accuracy and the lock busted open. He stepped inside and tried the light switch. Dead. The prick had cut off the power in his own home, so he could skulk around in the dark.

Finn waited for his eyes to adjust to the gloom.

'It's really dark, Uncle Finn,' whined Kurt, lingering on the doorstep.

'Man up, Kurt. You're a Finnegan. Finnegans aren't afraid of the dark.'

'No, no, no, of course not,' said Kurt, a little too quickly. Finn hated that his nephew was so feeble. Too much like his parents. Not enough Finnegan in his blood. 'But I can't see.'

'Then get your arse in here. Your eyes will adjust.' His nephew shuffled inside, eyes warily scanning the corners of the hallway, and the dark void at the top of the stairs. 'And shut that door behind you.'

Turn to page 361.

Chapter 28

But the blow never came.

Ted stood blinking in confusion, mouth agape. The point of a kitchen knife was sticking out of his chest. Instantly, his arms went slack and the baton fell. The knife was abruptly yanked out of his back, and his legs collapsed beneath him.

Sophie stood behind where Ted had been standing, knife in hand. It was the same knife Jack had used on Joan.

Ted stared up at her, spluttering, presumably trying to mouth the word, 'Why?'

Sophie answered by stabbing him a bunch more times. She seemed to be enjoying herself. Jack knew that feeling.

When she was finished, Sophie stood up and brushed aside a strand of hair from her head, which left a smear of blood on her forehead, like a bandana.

'Alone at last,' she said, with a happy sigh.

'Thank you?' said Jack, then managed to ask the question which Ted had only mouthed. 'Why?'

'Two's company but three is a crowd,' said Sophie, as if that explained the matter. 'I thought it was time to ditch the third wheel.'

'Couldn't agree more,' said Jack, warily, unsure where this was going.

Sophie stared at him, unblinking, smiling, her head tilted slightly to one side, as though admiring a piece of art. This went on for some time. Goosebumps rose on Jack's arms.

Eventually, he said, 'Are you waiting for me to speak?'

'No, no,' laughed Sophie. 'Just appreciating your eyes. Such lovely eyes. I spotted them at the Christmas party last year. I've thought about them ever since.'

'Oh.' Jack blushed. 'Erm, that's very nice of you.'

'I often wondered whether I should tell you about Joan and Ted,' she said. 'But I thought you might get angry with me, shoot the messenger. I couldn't stand you being angry with me.'

'Okay,' said Jack, slowly, squirming in his seat.

She still hadn't blinked.

'I also thought about trying to start up an affair with you,' she said, dreamily. 'After all, your wife was at it, so why not you?' She shook her head. 'But I thought, not my Jack, he's much too good to be unfaithful, even to a cheating B-word like Joan.'

Behind his back, Jack writhed against the handcuffs. The comment about his lovely eyes made him nervous. She was still holding the enormous kitchen knife, now wet with two people's blood.

'But finally we can be together!' declared Sophie, loudly. 'The obstacles are removed. You killed one, I killed one. A relationship is all about sharing the problems that life throws your way.'

'Relationship?'

'You and I. Finally.'

'Sophie, I'm really very flattered but – ' He instantly regretted saying 'but.' Immediately, Sophie's face darkened and her knife-hand twitched. 'I've just gotten out of a serious relationship.' Understatement. 'I need some time by myself.'

Plus, I don't really know anything about you. I barely remembered your name.

'No,' said Sophie, firmly.

'No?'

'I can't waste any more time waiting for you. This is it now. Jack and Sophie, together at last.'

'But – '

'And if you're having second thoughts,' she began, pointing the knife tip at his chest. 'Then I'll tell the police all about the murders we committed. I know quite a few police officers, funnily enough.'

Jack fell silent.

'But I'm sure it won't come to that,' she added, brightening. 'Now, let's get you out of those handcuffs. We have two bodies to bury.'

She squealed with excitement and clapped her hands so suddenly that Jack almost had a heart attack.

'Our first date!'

THE END

Chapter 29

But the blow never came.

A small knife appeared over Ted's shoulder and reached across the front of his neck.

'Wha – '

In one neat movement, the knife was drawn back and Ted's throat split open, instantly gushing out a deluge of blood, most of which went over Jack.

More for the collection.

Ted dropped his baton in shock and clamped both hands over the gaping slit, gasping and gargling. He staggered one-eighty degrees to face his attacker. There stood Sophie, his fellow officer, a look of grim satisfaction on her face.

She darted in again with her little knife and punctured Ted a dozen more times. She then shoved his lifeless body aside where it thudded into the television cabinet. She spat on his body for good measure.

Ted's dead, baby. Ted's dead.

'Erm, thanks?' said Jack.

Sophie gave a humourless laugh. 'Don't thank me yet, you piece of shit. I didn't do that for you.'

Jack realised with a sickening lurch that the small knife she was holding wasn't from his kitchen. She must have brought it with her. Did she carry a knife around with her all the time? A police officer?

'I couldn't let Ted have all the fun,' she said, eyes gleaming at Jack. 'I loved her too you know. Joan. If I'd ever thought she would swing my way then I might have told her. Instead, I had to watch her from afar. Staying married to someone who didn't appreciate her. Fooling around with a prick like Ted.'

Sophie retrieved a small package from inside her jacket. It was a bundle of neatly-folded black cloth, about the size of a clutch-bag. She set it on the sofa next to Jack.

'What are you doing?' asked Jack, eyeing the package.

Sophie ignored him and slowly started to unfold the cloth. 'Joan deserved better than both of you. She would have been happy with me.'

Inside the package was a collection of sharp little blades. Each was clean and polished, clearly well-cared for, lovingly so.

'What is that?'

'My pumpkin-carving kit.'

Sophie sized Jack up, prodding his stomach, before tracing a finger over his torso. Her evaluation done, she returned to her kit and carefully selected a pointy scalpel.

'Wait, stop,' pleaded Jack.

'I always did love Halloween,' said Sophie. 'Now, hold still. I'm going to make myself a Jack-o'-lantern.'

THE END

Chapter 30

' – rrrrrrgh! Soph, do something!'

Ted frowned. 'Soph?'

Before the bigger man could pull out the knife to stab Jack again, Sophie rushed forward and whacked Ted on the temple with her baton. The blow landed with a nasty cracking sound. Ted staggered sideways, dazed, but didn't go down. Sophie ditched the baton with a curse. Instead, she yanked the knife out of Jack's leg in one abrupt tug.

'Owowow!' screamed Jack, in a white-hot burst of agony. 'What the hell?'

'Trying to save your life, love,' said Sophie, charging forward and plunging the knife into Ted's heart before he could gather his wits to retaliate.

Now it was Ted's turn to scream. 'What the fuck?'

Sophie planted a hand on Ted's shoulder and drove him to the ground. When he was sprawled on his back, Sophie stomped a foot firmly on his chest and leant harder on the knife.

'You and Joan weren't the only police officers having an affair,' she replied.

Ted's eyes widened in realisation, or perhaps they widened because the life was leaving them. Within moments, they were glassy and bulging, housing a pained, faraway look.

Ted was gone.

'Christ, Sophie,' cried Jack. 'Why didn't you do that before he attacked me?'

'I had to wait until he put the knife down,' she said, dusting herself off.

'He put the knife down in me!'

'Only in your leg.'

'Only? It hurt!'

'Not as much as what I did to Ted.'

'Fair point.'

'You're welcome, by the way.'

'Handcuffs, Sophie. Get them off me. We need to do something about my leg.'

'Manners cost nothing, dear.'

'Sophie! Please, thank you, whatever! I'm bleeding out, here.'

'Alright, alright.' She retrieved the key from Ted's

belt. 'Ugh, so much blood.' As she tackled the handcuffs, she said, 'Anyway, Jack. What happened with Joan? Murdering her wasn't part of our plan.'

'I lost my temper.'

'So I see.'

'Do you still want to be with me?'

'Yes, dear. It would take more than murdering your wife to stop me loving you. Do you still love me, after seeing what I did to Ted?'

'More than ever.'

Click. The handcuffs fell away. Jack shook some life into his wrists.

'So what do you want to do?' asked Sophie. 'Sew up your leg? Bury the bodies? Mop up the blood?'

'None are exactly how I pictured our first night of freedom together.'

'Then you make a suggestion.'

Jack looked longingly at his paused horror show, before turning to Sophie.

'Netflix and chill?'

THE END

Chapter 31

' – rrrrrrrgh!'

Jack convulsed in agony. Pain sensors were blaring up and down his body, screeching a siren in his head. And that was just one stab. Jack spared a thought for Joan, albeit a fleeting one, and what she must have suffered at his hands.

The knife stung like a bastard. To make it worse, Ted still hadn't pulled it out.

'Oh shit, oh shit,' rambled Ted, clearly realising he had crossed a line, despite his big talk about torturing Jack moments ago. He staggered backwards, cupping his mouth in horror.

Sophie reacted instantly. 'Right, this has gone far enough. I'm calling it in.' She gripped the radio on her jacket. 'Despatch, this is Officer – '

'No!' Ted snatched Sophie's wrist away from her radio, more in fear than anger. 'Don't, please.'

'Let go of my wrist,' she demanded, but Ted held on.

'I'll lose my job, Sophie.'

'Never mind your job, Ted. You're in danger of losing your mind. You need help.'

'He deserves this,' shouted Ted. 'He butchered Joan.'

'Let go of my wrist, right now.'

Ted paused, thinking. 'No.'

'No?' Her eyes showed the first glimmer of panic. She tried to pull herself free of her colleague's grip, but he wasn't letting her go.

'I can't let you report this,' he said. 'Not before I get justice for Joan.'

Ted slowly drew his baton with his other hand. Seeing this, Sophie struggled to pull her wrist free more desperately. 'Ted, stop,' she said, her voice becoming shrill. 'You're not thinking clearly.'

'I'm not going to prison over this piece of shit,' he continued, gesturing with his drawn baton.

'Ted, don't!'

He raised the baton over his head. Sophie urgently reached for her mace –

Ted was quicker.

The first strike was enough to stun Sophie into

dropping her mace. The second, third and fourth brought Sophie to the floor. Everything after that was just Ted being thorough. Or insane. Jack knew the feeling well.

And he was about to know it again.

Now!

Jack limped forward and stabbed the kitchen knife into Ted's upper back.

'Garrrgh!'

Jack stepped away, leaving the knife dug deep in Ted's back. Ted remained on his feet but he was frozen in place, the wound ravaging his nervous system. Eventually, he rotated in a half-circle to address his attacker. Even that movement took time, Ted now only capable of jerky, mechanical movements, like a stop motion animation.

He gasped, 'How?'

Jack stood holding the kitchen knife that had been buried in his thigh. He had pulled it out himself. That had hurt immensely, but it was nothing compared to what Ted was going through.

'How did I get out of the handcuffs?' finished Jack.

Ted looked like he wanted to nod.

'I was married to a police officer for five years,' said Jack. 'Joan told me how to get out of handcuffs.'

Every police officer was taught the knack of undoing handcuffs without a key, in case they were ever disabled by a criminal and their own cuffs were used against them.

Ted spluttered, now looking like he wanted to say something. He crashed down onto his knees instead.

'You're wondering why she would tell me about the knack,' said Jack. 'I'm just a lowly civilian after all. Well, the thing about being married to a police officer is that handcuffs always get brought into the bedroom sooner or later. Best I know how to undo them to avoid a *Gerald's Game* situation.'

Jack's mood suddenly darkened.

'I'm sure you know what I'm talking about. I bet you and Joan used handcuffs in your little hotel meet-ups.'

Ted didn't deny it, though perhaps he was unable to shake his head. His eyes appeared to be pleading. Jack wasn't sure if it was a plea for his life, or a desire for Jack to end his pain.

But Jack wasn't quite done.

'Joan's death,' he began. 'It was on you. I want these to be the last words you hear. It was on you.'

Now, Jack was done. He limped forward and shove the knife straight through Ted's heart. The bigger man shuddered, gargled, and finally slumped forward. Jack's second ever kill and it only took two thrusts. He was learning.

After Ted's body had stopped twitching, Jack sank into the sofa with a heavy sigh. He was exhausted. His attention wandered to Sophie's body. Perhaps he should have stabbed Ted before the bigger man had killed Sophie, but he couldn't trust Sophie not to reach for her radio again. He had no choice, he told himself. Still, he supposed that meant her death was on his hands too.

'Three bodies to bury,' he said, wearily. He looked longingly at his paused horror show and reluctantly turned off the television.

Jack went to fetch his chainsaw.

THE END

Chapter 32

'Money!' said Jack, voice flooded with desperation. He grabbed the piggy bank kept by the front door. Joan and he emptied their loose change into the pig upon arriving home each day. Jack rapidly emptied the change into his hand. 'Money is better than food. You can take it to the shop and buy whatever you want. Chocolate, sweets, crisps, fizzy pop, magazines, toys, anything!'

'Crisps?' grunted the mummy.

'Pop?' said the skeleton.

'Hold out your hands again,' said Jack. 'Both hands. Cup them together.'

The three monsters did hold out their hands, though with more suspicion this time. Jack tipped a load of coins into each pair. He exhausted the entire piggy bank. There were some ten and twenty pence coins in the mix. Not a bad haul.

'There's a shop at the bottom of this cul-de-sac,' explained Jack. 'It should still be open. Why don't you go there now?' Then in a louder, pleading, panicking voice, 'Go there now! Go there now!'

The monsters appeared confused by the coins. The jack-o'-lantern sniffed them. The mummy lifted them to the side of its head like a conch shell, apparently expecting them to make a noise. The skeleton considered its coins thoughtfully, tilting its head to one side then the other.

'Have you not seen money before?' asked Jack.

The skeleton responded by scooping the coins into its mouth, throwing its head back, and swallowing them all in one go.

'I guess not,' said Jack, unblinking. 'They're not – They're not for eating!'

Then things got weird again.

The skeleton jerked painfully as the calcium-white of its bones transformed into silver-bronze metal. Within moments, it fell still, frozen in place.

The jack-o'-lantern and mummy inspected their colleague, now reduced to a gleaming metallic statue. The jack-o'-lantern gave the skeleton's head an experimental rap with its knuckles. The mummy waved a bandaged hand in front of the skeleton's eyeless sockets. Neither action prompted the monster to move.

'Trick!' moaned the mummy.

'Trick!' hissed the jack-o'-lantern.

'It's not my fault!' cried Jack. 'Your mate wasn't supposed to eat the money.'

The jack-o'-lantern took a menacing step forward, the fire within its head glowing extra brightly. The mummy advanced too, loosening a bandage and holding it taut between both hands, ready to strangle Jack.

Thankfully, the effect on the skeleton didn't last much longer. The statuesque figure jerked violently. The metal receded from its bones, leaving only white once again.

'Trick,' shouted the skeleton, pointing a bony finger at Jack. The tip of the finger was filed into a sharp point.

'Wait, wait,' he pleaded. 'Give me another chance.'

Strike three, thought Jack.

Gum, fruit, money –

He only had one option left.

Give the monsters a weight loss bar, turn to page 76.

To explain the situation, turn to page 129.

Chapter 33

'Here you go!' said Jack, voice flooded with desperation. He held out three red apples. 'It wouldn't be Halloween without a few apples. You can bob for them later.'

'Apple?' grunted the skeleton.

'Bob?' said the mummy.

'Mine!' said the jack-o'-lantern, snatching an apple from Jack's hand. It held the apple to the jagged line that had been carved for its mouth.

Good luck shoving a whole apple through there, thought Jack.

But then the jack-o'-lantern's mouth miraculously opened wide and took a bite from the apple. And another and another and another.

'Omnomnomnom!'

Jack stared in disbelief.

The pumpkin swallowed the apple core afterwards with a big gulp.

'What the hell?' said Jack.

It couldn't be a real pumpkin, after all. The mouth had opened and closed like living flesh. A mask then? An animatronic mask?

But then things got weird.

The jack-o'-lantern groaned and clutched its stomach. It shuddered violently and its pumpkin-head started to redden, swell outwards and upwards, whilst a stem the size and thickness of a marker pen sprouted from the top of its head.

Jack gaped.

The jack-o'-lantern's pumpkin-head had transformed into an apple-head.

'What – What the – '

The other two trick-or-treaters turned to Jack and hissed at him.

'Trick,' said the skeleton, pointing an accusing bony finger.

'Trick,' repeated the mummy.

'No,' stammered Jack. 'I didn't know it would do that.'

The jack-o'-lantern shuddered again, prompting the reverse to happen. The apple-head reformed into its pumpkin-head through a series of violent jerks, leaving the jack-o'-lantern bent double, gasping.

'Trick,' it spat, pointing at Jack.

'Wait, wait,' he pleaded. 'Give me another chance.'

Strike three, thought Jack.

Gum, money, fruit –

He only had one option left.

Give the monsters a weight loss bar, turn to page 76.

To explain the situation, turn to page 129.

Chapter 34

'Money!' said Jack, voice flooded with desperation. He grabbed the piggy bank kept by the front door, into which he and Joan emptied their loose change upon arriving home each day. Jack was now rapidly emptying the change into his hand. 'Money is better than food. You can take it to the shop and buy whatever you want. Chocolate, sweets, crisps, fizzy pop, magazines, toys, anything!'

'Crisps?' grunted the mummy.

'Pop?' said the skeleton.

'Hold out your hands again,' said Jack. 'Both hands. Cup them together.'

The three monsters did hold out their hands – bandaged, skeletal and gloved – though with more suspicion this time. Jack tipped a load of coins into each pair. He exhausted the entire piggy bank. There were some ten and twenty pence coins in the mix. Not a bad haul.

'There's a shop at the bottom of this cul-de-sac,'

explained Jack. 'It should still be open. Why don't you go there now?' Then in a louder, pleading, panicky voice, 'Go there now! Go there now!'

The monsters appeared confused by the coins. The jack-o'-lantern sniffed them. The mummy lifted them to the side of its head like a conch shell, apparently expecting them to make a noise. The skeleton considered its coins thoughtfully, tilting its head to one side, then the other.

'Have you not seen money before?' asked Jack.

The skeleton responded by scooping the coins into its mouth and throwing its head back, swallowing them in one go.

'I guess not,' said Jack, unblinking. 'They're not – They're not for eating!'

Then things got weird again.

The skeleton jerked painfully as the calcium-white of its bones transformed into silver-bronze metal. Within moments, it fell still, frozen in place.

The jack-o'-lantern and mummy inspected their colleague, now a gleaming metallic statue. The jack-o'-lantern gave the skeleton's head an experimental rap with its knuckles. The mummy waved a bandaged hand in front of the skeleton's eyeless sockets. Neither action prompted their fellow monster to move.

'Trick!' moaned the mummy.

'Trick!' hissed the jack-o'-lantern.

'It's not my fault!' cried Jack. 'Your mate wasn't supposed to eat the money.'

The jack-o'-lantern took a menacing step forward, the fire within its head glowing extra brightly. The mummy advanced too, loosening a bandage and holding it taut between both hands, intending to strangle Jack.

Thankfully, the effect on the skeleton didn't last much longer. The statuesque figure jerked and the metal receded from its bones, leaving only white once again.

'Trick,' shouted the skeleton, pointing a bony finger at Jack. The tip of the finger was filed into a sharp point.

'Wait, wait,' he pleaded. 'Give me another chance.'

Strike three, thought Jack.

Gum, fruit, money –

He only had one option left.

Give the monsters a weight loss bar, turn to page 76.

To explain the situation, turn to page 129.

Chapter 35

The Wee Wise Weevil

by Joan Juniper

The wee wise weevil saw a sad house fly,
"Hello, house fly, why do you cry?"

"I'm plain, I'm lame, as pointless as can be!
Nothing is good about boring old me."

The wee wise weevil said, "That cannot be true.
Who would you rather be, if you were not you?"

"I wish I were a crane fly – that would be the best!
Their legs are super spindly, taller than the rest."
Yet the sad house fly gave a heavy sigh,
"Alas, I am too short to be a crane fly...

But why am I telling you? You're only wee,
How can a tiny weevil help a fly like me?"

The wee wise weevil said, "Please, let me try –"
But the sad house fly continued to cry.

"I'm bland, I'm bleak, as benign as can be!
Nothing is grand about boring old me.
I wish I were a butterfly – imagine such a thing!
To have beautiful patterns painted on each wing."
Yet the sad house fly gave another sigh,
"Alas, I am too drab to be a butterfly...
But why am I telling you? You're only wee,
How can a wincey weevil help a fly like me?"

The wee wise weevil said, "Stop, I can help –"
But the sad house fly continued to yelp.

"I'm dumb, I'm glum, as dreary as can be!
Nothing is cool about boring old me.
I wish I were a blow fly – then I would grin.
With bristles all over my shiny metal skin."
Yet the sad house fly gave a further sigh,

"Alas, I am too smooth to be a blow fly...
But why am I telling you? You're only wee,
How can a teeny weevil help a fly like me?"

The wee wise weevil said, "Wait, just a sec – "
But the sad house fly was a sobbing wreck.

"I'm drab, I'm grey, as shabby as can be!
Nothing is fun about boring old me.
I wish I were a fire fly – I'd put on a show!
Lighting the night with my luminescent glow."
Yet the sad house fly gave a final sigh,
"Alas, I am too dull to be a fire fly...
But why am I telling you? You're only wee,
How can a titchy weevil help a fly like me?"

The wee wise weevil said, "I may be wee,
But please dry your eyes and listen to me.
Come, house fly, hear what I have to say,
You are looking at this in the wrong way.
Don't be sad that you are unlike the rest,
Perhaps being a house fly is the best.
The crane fly is too tall to be you,

The butterfly is too colourful to be you,
The blow fly is too bristly to be you,
The fire fly is too bright to be you!"

The house fly wiped its multifaceted eyes,
And saw that the wee wise weevil was wise.
"I've never thought about it like that before..."
And the sad house fly was sad no more.
"I am glad we spoke, thanks for helping me,
Please do forgive me for calling you wee."

The wee wise weevil laughed, "But I *am* wee!
You see, being wee is what makes me, me!"

Chapter 36

Ding dong. Ding dong.

Jack would love to swing open the front door and scare the kids shitless. He would love to see the terror on their faces as he stood before them, crazy-eyed, covered in his wife's blood, maybe wielding the kitchen knife that he had put to use once already this evening. He would *especially* love to invite the relentless little fuckers into his house of horrors and stab some good manners into them.

But he had retained enough rational thought amidst his burgeoning insanity to realise that opening the front door would definitely end in his arrest and incarceration.

So Jack did the next best thing to dissuade any further trick-or-treaters. He stormed over to the bay window to remove the pumpkin, after which he would probably beat it to a pump with his bare hands in a deranged frenzy, such was his state of mind –

Only the pumpkin wouldn't budge.

'What?'

Jack tried again. No luck. It was stuck fast.

He grabbed it with both hands, and pulled and yanked and jerked.

'What the hell, Joan? Did you glue this thing on?'

Jack next planted his feet on the wall below the windowsill and pulled back with all his might, pushing with his legs, his entire weight urging the pumpkin to come free. The pumpkin didn't move an inch.

But Jack did. He lost his grip and landed on his backside in a rage.

'You fucking – '

Jack choked on his insult. The pumpkin was slowly rotating of its own accord. When the pumpkin's carved features were fully facing Jack, it burst into flame.

'Oh shit!'

Its grin started to widen, as though it were made of human flesh and not marrow.

And then it spoke.

'You always did have a temper,' said the pumpkin.

'What?' said Jack, scrambling backwards on his arse. 'Who – ?'

'Now it's my turn to be hot-headed.'

The flaming pumpkin levitated from the windowsill and shot towards Jack like a cannonball. Jack threw himself backwards just in time to avoid a face full of fire. He spun around, expecting a repeat attack, but the flaming pumpkin had been caught by a figure standing behind him.

The figure was female in shape but her substance was ethereal. Jack could see through her body into the kitchen which remained drenched in blood. Her head was even more disturbing, in that she didn't have one.

But not for long. She raised the flaming pumpkin and planted it firmly on the stump of her neck.

'You picked a bad night to kill me,' said the pumpkin.

'Kill you? Joan?' He stammered, cowering back. 'You're a ghost?'

'No, not a ghost,' said Joan. She rose up from the

ground, hovering over Jack, and the flames engulfing her pumpkin-head grew bigger. 'You killed me in a fit of violence and anger and jealousy.'

'I'm sorry,' he sobbed.

'That sort of outburst doesn't create ghosts. Not on Halloween.'

'What are you then?'

'A poltergeist.'

Joan grabbed Jack by the throat and flung him into a wall.

It was the first of many.

THE END

Chapter 37

'Wait, wait, wait, listen to me!' pleaded Jack. 'I'm trying my best to find you a treat. Can't you see that I'm trying?'

The three monsters stopped advancing but their anger was not doused by Jack's words.

'Sugar,' demanded the skeleton.

'There is no sugar in the house,' said Jack. 'I told you.'

'Sugar,' repeated the jack-o'-lantern.

'I don't have any,' said Jack. 'There must be other things you like.'

'Sugar,' groaned the mummy.

'I – don't – have – any!' shouted Jack, emphasising each word. 'No sugar, none, all gone.' He made frantic swiping gestures with his arms. 'Gone, gone, gone. Finished. No more.'

The three monsters stared at him silently, then the skeleton quietly asked, 'What happened to the sugar?'

Jack gulped. He could still taste it on his teeth.

'Erm.'

To lie, turn to page 131.

To tell the truth, turn to page 133.

Chapter 38

'I gave it all to trick-or-treaters,' he lied. 'You got here too late.'

The monsters stared, distrustfully.

'All?' said the skeleton.

'Yes,' said Jack, sorely remembering that he had eaten half of the treats himself.

The skeleton sniffed. The jack-o'-lantern and mummy joined in.

'What are you doing?' asked Jack, nervously.

Their sniffs became louder, longer, more zealous.

Oh God, realised Jack. *They can smell it on me.*

'Liar!' shouted the skeleton, levelling a damning finger at Jack.

The mummy's bandages shot forward and wrapped around Jack's wrists, neck and torso. They yanked Jack forward and he landed heavily on his kneecaps.

'No, stop!'

Jack was bound and genuflecting in front of his tormentors, utterly at their mercy. His head was level with the diminutive skeleton, who grabbed his face with ice-cold, bony fingers. Its grip was like a vice on his jaw. Despite lacking a nose, the skeleton leaned in close and smelt Jack's breath.

'Sugar!' it announced in triumph. 'Inside you.'

'No, no, no, no, no, no,' murmured Jack, sobbing.

'Inside your stomach,' said the skeleton. 'In your blood.'

The three monsters bared their teeth, drooling, and pounced, eager to feast on the Jack-sized chocolate bar in front of them.

They tore off the wrapper first.

THE END

Chapter 39

'I ate half of the treats myself,' confessed Jack, head bowed.

'And the other half?' asked the skeleton.

'I poured the rest into some trick-or-treater's bag,' explained Jack, swallowing anxiously. 'A teenager. He got here right before you did.'

'Truth?' asked the skeleton.

'Truth,' said Jack, solemnly.

The three monsters exchanged glances before huddling together, conversing quickly in that strange, chittering language that he had heard them use earlier that evening. Jack watched, heart pounding, palms sweating, as they discussed his fate.

Eventually, their chatter died away and the skeleton sagely nodded his head. The three creatures reformed their line, like a monstrous jury.

Jack wasn't sure if he wanted to hear their

verdict.

To run inside, turn to page 135.

To hear their verdict, turn to page 137.

Chapter 40

Jack cut his losses and slammed the door in their faces.

Immediately, he heard angry snarls and attacks against the door. There was a horrible scratching noise, which Jack assumed was the skeleton furiously slashing at the wood with its sharp fingers. This was followed by a thud-thud-thud against the frosted glass window fitted into the top half of the door. Jack could make out the mummy's serpentine bandages jabbing away at the glass. It was already starting to splinter.

Then the glass shattered completely as a ball of flame blasted right through it.

'Shit!'

Jack dived backwards. He narrowly avoided getting his face burnt off. Damn jack-o'-lantern.

'Forget this.'

Jack doubted his wooden front door would hold

back three demons for much longer, but he put the safety chain on anyway, before sprinting further into his house.

Where to hide? Where to hide?

To hide in the kitchen, turn to page 139.

To hide in the study, turn to page 142.

Chapter 41

'We will find the teenager,' said the skeleton. 'He can't have gotten far.'

'You're going to steal his chocolate?' said Jack.

'We can gut you and take the chocolate out of your stomach, if you'd prefer?' said the skeleton, darkly.

Jack turned pale and said nothing.

'Thought so,' said the skeleton. The jack-o'-lantern gave him a nudge. 'Ah, that's right. We are grateful for your honesty. As a reward, we would like to offer you something.'

'You would?' said Jack. Now it was his turn to stare distrustfully. 'What something?'

The skeleton grinned. It was a skull, so it was always grinning, but it seemed to Jack that it was grinning even more now, particularly when it asked its question.

'Trick or treat?'

Trick, turn to page 149.

Treat, turn to page 145.

Chapter 42

Jack treated to the kitchen, the furthest room from the front door. It was still a mess from when he had cooked dinner, but at least that meant there was an arsenal of pots, pans and blades on the worktop. He could defend himself.

Jack reached for a frying pan and blade.

'Who am I kidding?'

A frying pan and carving knife weren't going to save him. These were demons, for crying out loud. Three of them.

He considered the back door. He could keep running. Surely, he was faster than a lumbering mummy, but what about the other two? Or was space a relative concept for the monsters? Could they conjure weird vortexes, or whatever, so they could cover great distances in a single step?

Knock knock.

'Oh, fuck.'

Well, it was irrelevant now. The jack-o'-lantern stood at the back door, knocking with one hand and waving cheerfully with the other. *Oh, look, and the door isn't locked.* The jack-o'-lantern stepped into the kitchen, looking pleased as punch. At the same time, the kitchen door thudded open and the skeleton strode in.

Both monsters lined up in front of Jack before turning to the kitchen door, awaiting the final member of their band. Eventually, *eventually*, the mummy staggered in, arms outstretched, groaning. It took its place in the line-up. All three monsters turned to Jack.

'Hello again,' said Jack, feebly.

The three monsters glared, their eyes boring into him. Jack cowered on the other side of his kitchen island. He was cornered. Nowhere to run. Outnumbered three-to-one.

Well, three-to-two, realised Jack.

He spotted his only ally in the battle to come. Of course. Nobody was alone nowadays.

After all, the year was –

If your mobile number ends in an odd number, turn to page 154.

If your mobile number ends in an even number, turn to page 157.

Chapter 43

Jack sped upstairs to the study, for no other reason than it was Joan's study really, and he was missing his wife right now.

Books lined the walls. Joan enjoyed having her own space to read, somewhere to store her countless paperbacks, which was fine by Jack because it gave him free reign over the television downstairs. He was more of a film enthusiast anyway.

Jack locked the door behind him. It didn't block out the sound of the monsters attacking his front door. He realised he might never see his wife again. He felt very alone.

'You're never alone if you have books,' Joan had often said to him.

Jack scanned the bookshelves, looking for companionship. The shelves were brimming with books that he had never read, never heard of, and never wanted to read, yet Joan had digested them all, some on several occasions judging by their creased spines. Jack struggled with books. He lacked the concentration. It was one of the many ways in which he and Joan were different.

And *there* was another way.

Joan's Bible sat on the bookshelf. She was a devout Christian. Jack was a firm atheist, mostly because it was less effort. Evidence of Joan's faith was clearly evidenced by her copy of the Bible. It was an illustrated Bible that she had been given as a little girl. She had read it so many times that its spine had almost fully crumbled away.

Jack thought about picking it up and embracing his wife's faith. If demons were real, then why not angels too?

But he also spied his wife's favourite book, every bit as fervently read as her Bible. Joan had been reading the book when they had first met in a coffee shop. She had taken it on their honeymoon. Nothing reminded him of his wife more than that curious blue book.

A loud crash announced that the front door had been kicked open. The monsters were in the house.

Immediately, their cries for 'Sugar!' carried upstairs.

Jack panicked.

To grab the Bible, turn to page 160.

To grab Joan's favourite book, turn to page 162.

Chapter 44

'Treat,' said Jack instantly.

He wasn't foolish enough to invite three monsters to trick him on Halloween.

'Very well,' said the skeleton, nodding to the mummy.

The mummy reached into its filthy bandages where its midriff should have been. It rummaged around, searching for something. When it withdrew its hand, it was holding a sphere, wrapped in yet more filthy bandages. The mummy ceremoniously unravelled the bandages to reveal a flawless glass ball.

Not glass, he told himself. *Crystal. A crystal ball.*

The mummy offered the ball to Jack.

'Erm, thank you,' he said. 'Is this my treat?'

'Look,' groaned the mummy.

Jack gazed into the ball. Images appeared inside, much like a video playing on his phone. He saw two figures inside the ball. They were having sex in a bed he didn't recognise, but he did recognise the figures.

Joan and Ted.

His wife and her work colleague.

Jack had always suspected, but he hated himself for being jealous, riddled with suspicion, awash with insecurity, so he cast his envy and paranoia aside. He tried not to dwell on why his wife was going out on Halloween to supposedly meet a friend he had never heard of.

'This isn't a treat!' said Jack, thrusting the ball back at the mummy.

'No,' said the skeleton.

'I don't want to know that my wife is out there having sex right now.'

'Not now.'

'Sorry?'

'The events in the ball took place earlier,' explained the skeleton.

'Well, whatever,' said Jack. 'It's still not a treat.'

'No, here is your treat.'

The jack-o'-lantern stepped forward, holding out its hollow pumpkin in two hands. Jack had assumed the pumpkins were their version of a plastic Aldi bag, a repository to collect their sweets when door-knocking.

The jack-o'-lantern, giggling to itself, whipped off the top of the pumpkin with a flourish. Jack cried out in shock. Looking up at him from inside the hollow pumpkin was Ted. His eyes were vacant, his mouth slack.

'What the fuck?' said Jack. 'You cut off his head?'

The jack-o'-lantern nodded enthusiastically.

'You cut off his head,' repeated Jack, beginning to smile to himself. 'Hah! Take that, you fucking prick. That's what you get for fucking my wife.' He spat on the decapitated head. 'I hope it hurt, you fucker.'

Jack puffed out his chest in triumph, eyes wild. Ted might have seduced his wife, but at least Jack's head was still attached to his neck. Jack had the last laugh –

'My turn.'

The mummy lumbered forward, holding its own pumpkin.

'What?' said Jack, eyeing the second pumpkin with dread. 'No, don't.'

The skeleton and jack-o'-lantern watched Jack carefully, eager to drink in his remorse. Meanwhile, the mummy stoically removed the top of its pumpkin. Jack knew what would be inside.

Joan.

His wife's head looked up at him. The horror tore his mind to ribbons.

'Put it back!

Put it back!

Put it back!

Put it back!

Put it back!

Put it back!

Put it back!

Put –

THE END

Chapter 45

'Trick,' said Jack slowly.

He didn't trust the monsters. If he'd said treat then it would turn into a punishment, undoubtedly, so he gave the answer they would least expect.

'Very well,' said the skeleton, nodding to the mummy.

The mummy reached into its filthy bandages where its midriff should have been. It rummaged around, searching. When it withdrew its hand, it was holding a sphere, wrapped in yet more filthy bandages. The mummy ceremoniously unravelled the bandages to reveal a flawless glass ball.

Not glass, he told himself. *Crystal. A crystal ball.*

The mummy offered the ball to Jack.

'Erm, thank you,' he said, accepting is cautiously. He waited for the trick. Was it going to burst in his hands like a water balloon? Were a bunch of scrunched-up toy snakes going to pop out at him like one of those trick cans?

'Look,' said the mummy.

Jack gazed into the ball. Images appeared inside, much like a video playing on his phone. He saw two figures inside the ball. They were having sex in a bed he didn't recognise, but he did recognise the figures.

Joan and Ted.

His wife and her work colleague.

Jack had always suspected, but he hated himself for being jealous, riddled with suspicion, awash with insecurity, so he cast his envy and paranoia aside. He tried not to dwell on why his wife was going out on Halloween to supposedly meet a friend.

The fury and grief inside him scrambled over each other to elicit their reaction first –

But Jack had a thought.

'Ah, wait,' said Jack. 'I said trick. This is a trick, isn't it? This is all fake. You have conjured this up to mess with me.' Jack thrust the ball back at the mummy. The three monsters stared at him silently and his confidence waned. 'It is a trick, right?'

'No,' said the skeleton. 'That was real. We wanted to repay your honesty with another truth.'

Jack floundered. 'So my wife – my wife has been cheating on me?'

'Yes.'

The emotions boiled up again within Jack, but the skeleton doused them with a distraction.

'Here is your trick,' it said, removing its jaunty top hat.

'What?'

The skeleton held its hat upside-down and waved its bony fingers over the open hole.

'Oh,' said Jack. 'A magic trick.' He sighed heavily. 'Look, I'm really not in the mood. Can you just leave me in peace?'

Though he couldn't tear his eyes away from the dark, gaping hole of the top hat, and the mesmerising dance of the skeleton's fingers over the void.

'Are you going to pull out a rabbit?'

Without warning, the three monsters started chanting:

> *'You can't cheat without a head,*
> *You can't cheat when you're dead.*

No more cheating in your bed,
No more cheating for poor old Ted!'

On the last word, the skeleton reached into its hat and pulled out a decapitated head. Jack shouted in shock and jerked backwards. It was Ted. His eyes were wide and vacant, his mouth agape, tongue lolling. The cut on his neck was rough and jagged. It hadn't been a quick decapitation.

'What the fuck?' said Jack. 'You cut off his head?'

The skeleton nodded.

'You cut off his head,' repeated Jack, beginning to smile to himself. 'Hah! Take that, you fucking prick. That's what you get for fucking my wife.' He spat on the decapitated head. 'I hope it hurt, you fucker.'

Jack puffed out his chest in triumph, eyes wild. Ted might have seduced his wife, but at least Jack's head was still attached to his neck. Jack had the last laugh –

'Again!' squealed the jack-o'-lantern, giggling enthusiastically.

'Wait, what?' said Jack.

The   skeleton   dropped   Ted's   head

unceremoniously on the doorstep. It resumed wiggling its fingers over the empty hat.

'No, stop,' said Jack, dreading what was coming. 'One trick is enough. No more. Please.'

The chanting began a second time.

'You can't cheat on your own,
You can't cheat all alone.
No more sex talk on the phone,
No more cheating for poor old – '

Jack covered his ears and fell to his knees. His mind snapped seven ways at once.

'Don't say it!

Don't say it!

Don't say it!

Don't say it!

Don't say it!

Don't –

THE END

Chapter 46

The year was 2019.

Most houses around here had a smart speaker.

'Alexa,' said Jack. 'I need your help.'

The cylindrical speaker awoke with its signature corona of blue light.

'Sure. How can I help?'

'Erm. Good question, actually.'

The three monsters advanced slowly, toying with Jack. They could see he was out of options. The jack-o'-lantern grinned a fiery grin, the skeleton flexed its sharp fingers, and strips of the mummy's bandages wriggled in the air like tentacles.

'Sugar!' they chorused. It became a maniacal mantra. 'Sugar! Sugar! Sugar!'

'Alexa, how do you exorcise a demon?'

'I'm sorry. I don't know that one.'

'Alexa, help. These monsters are about to mash me to pieces.'

'Playing Monster Mash by Bobby Pickett on Spotify.'

'No!'

'They did the mash! They did the moooonster mash. The monster mash! It was a graveyard smash –
'

'This isn't helping!' cried Jack.

The jack-o'-lantern sucked in breath, readying a fireball. Jack swore and ducked behind his kitchen island just in time. The ball of fire blasted the island into smouldering debris.

Immediately, the mummy's bandages whipped forward and tightened around Jack's wrists, neck and torso, before yanking him through the fiery remains. They deposited him choking and hurting on the kitchen tiles at their feet.

The skeleton grasped Jack's jaw in one hand and dragged him into a kneeling position. It pointed its razor-sharp bone of an index finger at Jack's eye, before pulling back its arm, like an archer drawing a bowstring. Jack saw what was going to happen. It was going to plunge its finger through his eyeball, into his brain.

'Alexa,' he croaked, struggling against the bandage around his throat.

'It was a graveyard smash – '

Damn thing. It knew every song ever recorded, yet here was Jack, about to die listening to the Monster Mash. What's worse, his fearsome tormentors actually seemed to be enjoying the song. At the very least, Jack should have requested a song that they didn't like. A final middle finger to the monsters before dying.

Wait.

Every song ever recorded.

A song they don't like.

That's it.

Turn to page 230.

Chapter 47

The year was 2039.

Every house around here had a smart speaker.

'Alexa,' said Jack. 'I need your help.'

The cylindrical speaker awoke with its signature corona of blue light.

'Sure. How can I help?'

'Exorcise these demons.'

'Would you like me to play your exercise playlist?'

'No!'

Stupid Alexa. Thirty years in people's homes and they still hadn't perfected her hearing.

The three monsters advanced slowly, toying with Jack. They could see he was out of options. The jack-o'-lantern grinned a fiery grin, the skeleton flexed its sharp fingers, and strips of the mummy's bandages wriggled in the air like tentacles.

'Sugar!' they chorused. It became a maniacal mantra. 'Sugar! Sugar! Sugar!'

'Alexa, how do you exorcise a demon?' said Jack, enunciating every word.

'Would you like me to download Ordained Skill?'

'Ordained? Like a priest?'

'That's right.'

Jack frowned. Did he?

'Erm, yes?'

'Downloading Ordained Skill.'

'Please be – '

Jack was going to say 'quick' but he could see the skeleton levelling one of its bony hands at Jack. All four sharp fingers pointed at his head like a quartet of darts.

'Shit!'

Jack snatched up a frying pan from the counter and covered his face. The bony fingertips pinged off the flying pan. Each left a scratch, a dent or both.

That could have been my face, realised Jack.

The skeleton wasted no time in raising its other hand. This time it aimed much lower and fired into Jack's thigh.

'Ow!' he screamed, falling to the ground in agony. The fingertip bones were lodged deep into his flesh.

He could only see their white bases, and even those were soon lost to the gurgling blood that rushed out of the entry wounds.

'Get over here,' demanded the skeleton. The mummy's bandages obliged, whipping forward and taking hold of Jack. They dragged him across the floor, a streak of blood left in his wake. The bandages deposited Jack at the monsters' feet.

'Me!' said the jack-o'-lantern, barging forward and towering over him. The fire inside its pumpkin-head glowed brightly. Its carved mouth curved upwards in a grin.

Turn to page 234.

Chapter 48

Jack grabbed the Bible and hugged it tightly to his chest. He had no idea how to pray but he fudged his way through it.

'Dear God,' he began. 'Please send help. There are three monsters at my door, probably sent by your adversary downstairs. Any help from your side of the clouds would be much appreciated right now.' Then, his voice wavering, 'Please, God, I want to live. I want to see my wife again.'

Jack could hear the monsters snarling and shouting downstairs, followed by his front door slamming shut. He was trapped inside the house with them.

'Oh my god, oh my god, oh my god, please, I know I've not been a faithful follower, but my wife has prayed enough for the both of us. Joan? You know Joan, right?' There were footsteps on the stairs. 'Thoughtful, selfless, police officer Joan? Prays nightly, looks after the community, gives money to charity, writes poems about insects for her little nieces and nephews. Named after Joan of Arc, who you *definitely* know. She was a saint, right? Can't you send me a saint?'

Something knock-knock-knocked on the locked study door.

'Too late,' said Jack, hugging the Bible even tighter. He waited to hear the words 'Trick or treat?' or more demands for sugar.

Instead, a gruff voice said, 'Are you going to let me in, or do I need to boot this door open?'

It was a man's voice, definitely not a monster.

'Erm, who is it?'

'Saint Eustace Hubertus,' said the voice. 'I was sent here to help.'

'It worked?' said Jack, amazed. He stared at the Bible in his hands. 'Praying actually worked?'

The door burst inwards.

'Hey!' said Jack.

'Too slow,' said Eustace, stepping into the study.

Turn to page 263.

Chapter 49

Jack reached for Joan's copy of *The Sheriff* by some guy called Simon Fairbanks. It sounded like a western and the front cover looked like *Lion King* fan-fiction, but apparently it was a fantasy novel. A short one too.

Joan had all twelve of the Nephos novels, but it was this first one, *The Sheriff*, which she came back to time after time. Perhaps it was a nostalgia thing because she had discovered it as a little girl, long before they started churning out the film adaptations which Jack still hadn't seen somehow.

Jack hugged the book tightly to his chest and thought of Joan. She had spent hours reading and re-reading *The Sheriff*. Its pages were full of her fingerprints, its every word had been devoured by her eyes, committed to her mind, whilst the story itself had drifted into her imagination, feeding it, rewarding it for her dedication.

Joan and the book had a special bond which Jack had never managed to achieve with a film. As such, the book was the next best thing to having Joan here herself in his final moments –

The study started shaking.

Oh, god, what are the monsters doing now?

He hugged the book tighter. Books tumbled from the shelves around him. The lightbulb above started swinging madly. Jack sunk to the floor and scurried under the desk. Duck and cover. If it works against earthquakes, maybe it would protect him from the demons too.

'Joan, I love you,' he said.

Pretty solid last words, he thought.

The rest of the books exploded from the shelves, heralding the arrival of a tall figure who staggered out of the bookshelf, as though it were a doorway.

'What?' stammered Jack.

He stared at the figure in utter astonishment. He was less surprised by the manner of its arrival than he was by its appearance. The figure was a six-foot, half-man-half-lion, decked out in black and silver armour, equipped with a shield and a big fuck-off sword.

'What on Earth?' said Jack.

'What on Nephos?' replied the lion man.

The lion noticed Jack under the table. The only thing preventing Jack from having a fear-induced heart attack was the lion's own confusion, which matched his own. It seemed just as confused by its sudden arrival as Jack.

'Wait, did you say Earth?' the lion man asked.

'Erm, yes?'

'This is Earth?

'Where else would we be?'

The lion pulled Jack out from under the table and fixed him with an urgent stare. 'Did you bring me here?'

'What? No!' Although the lion *did* look familiar. He had also said 'Nephos' just now, which rang a bell. 'At least, I don't think so.'

The lion unhanded Jack and stepped back, taking a calming breath. 'What is your name?'

'Jack. Who are you?'

'Denebola.'

'Denna what now?'

'Just call me Sheriff.'

Turn to page 238.

Chapter 50

Jack vomited.

'No, don't!' cried Eustace.

A jet of black, viscous, noxious liquid gushed forth, splattering the grass.

Balam pulled back his head – all three of them – and laughed. When Balam laughed, it wasn't just the sound of a man, but the chorus of a menagerie. The bull snorted, the ram bleated, the bear roared, the snake hissed, and the hawk cawed.

Eustace shook his head, his face fraught with concern.

'Better out than in,' said Jack, weakly.

'Not on this occasion. That Jäger was your tribute to me. Faith fuel. I needed that to boost my divine powers. Now they're waning.'

Jack could see it was true. Eustace's glowing white halo had dimmed to a pale grey.

'I'm sorry, Eustace.' Jack considered the

regurgitated Jäger puddle. 'Can't you, like, roll in it or something?'

Eustace gave Jack a dark look.

'I guess not. Well, at least you still have your – '

The hawk dived through the air and snatched Eustace's bow from his hands.

'Hey!'

The hawk swooped back to its master and dropped the bow into Balam's human hands. The demon snapped the bow over his knee. Eustace clutched his chest in remorse. Jack was more preoccupied with the fact that Balam was now standing on his own two feet.

'Wait, where is the bear?'

An enormous growl erupted behind Jack and Eustace. A heavy paw cuffed each of them over the head. Their skulls knocked together.

Blackness followed.

Turn to page 271.

Chapter 51

'No, I don't believe in God,' confessed Jack.

Eustace sighed.

'But I believe in what I can see,' added Jack. 'I have no doubt that those three creatures are from the darkest pit of Hell, and that glowing halo of yours isn't held up by string. So yeah, it stands to reason that there is a God.'

Eustace shook his head. 'That's not good enough. Faith isn't about reason. It's about belief. I need you to truly believe.'

'You do?' Jack startled. 'Wait, you're not ditching me, are you?'

'Of course not, I'm here to help, but I would be a lot stronger fighting alongside someone with faith. Faith is like fuel for a saint. Rocket fuel.'

'What does this mean?'

'It means I'll be no different from any other mortal being with a bow.'

'You have that floating halo,' said Jack, hopefully. 'No other mortal being has one of those.'

'I'll be sure to mention that when your three little friends are feasting on my guts.'

'I'm sorry, Eustace. My wife is the religious one.'

'Where is she?'

'Working.'

'Great.'

Jack felt useless. 'Is there nothing I can do to make you stronger?'

'I don't think so.'

'What if I pray really hard?'

Eustace scoffed. 'No, Jack.' Then his eyes widened. 'There is one thing we could try.'

'Name it.'

'There's a drink that might help.'

'A drink? What, like communion wine?'

'Not quite. A digestif.'

'A what?'

'Do you happen to have any Jägermeister in the house?'

Jack blinked. 'Jägermeister?'

'I mean, yeah, somewhere, but it's pretty nasty.'
Turn to page 185.

'Hell, no. I can't stand the stuff.' Turn to page 190.

Chapter 52

'Sword.'

'Are you sure?'

'I think so.'

'Have you wielded a blade before?'

'Nothing bigger than a bread knife.'

'Here. Hold the handle with two hands. Keep the blade low whenever you can to save your strength. When you are under attack, raise it in front of you and drive forward.'

Jack could barely lift the damn thing. 'Maybe you should keep it.'

'Don't worry about me. I'm just as lethal with my – Incoming!'

The Sheriff dived in front of Jack, his shield raised. An onslaught of sharp little bones flew at them like hailstones. The bones bounced off the shield and regrouped in the air, like a swarm of angry wasps. They swirled around, assessing another angle to attack from.

The Sheriff fended them off a second time, a third, positioning the shield to meet each attack, protecting them both.

Or so Jack thought.

One of the mummy's bandages lassoed his neck from behind and yanked him backwards. Jack choked and lost his balance, but luckily managed to keep his grip on the sword. The bandage reeled him in like a fish. It deposited him at the mummy's feet, where a nest of other bandages wrapped around his body. They pinned his arms to his sides, so he couldn't swing the sword. The bandage around his throat began to tighten.

Jack sought out the Sheriff but the lion-man still fended off attacks from the swarm of bones. Meanwhile, the jack-o'-lantern had found its feet. It marched past where Jack knelt choking. The demon's fiery eyes were fixed on the Sheriff's vulnerable back. A fireball crackled in the creature's carved mouth, ready to fire.

Oh no you don't.

Jack might not have a free hand, but he still had

his legs. He kicked out, tripping the jack-o'-lantern as it stormed past. The demon fell, its head jerking back, which unleashed the fireball at the wrong angle. It rocketed over the crouching Sheriff and blasted into the swarm of hovering bones. The skull, ribcage, fibula, and the rest, were thrown against the wall – itself receiving a scorching – before falling to the floor.

The Sheriff, now offered a brief respite from the skeleton, spun around and launched the shield like a discus. The circle of steel flew through the air with precision and severed the mummy's head from its shoulders. The bandages loosened immediately, tumbling away from Jack like paper chains.

'One down,' he gasped, rubbing his liberated neck.

The jack-o'-lantern picked itself up, already conjuring a second fireball to unleash at the Sheriff, who no longer had his shield. Jack had to do something.

Think fast, Jack.

To leap on the jack-o'-lantern, turn to page 192.

To use the sword, turn to page 194.

Chapter 53

'Shield, please.'

'Wise choice. Here.'

The Sheriff presented Jack with his shield. 'Put your arm through the strap.'

Jack did and the Sheriff let go. The weight of the shield toppled him forward.

'Whoa, this is heavy.'

'It is made from star-forged steel,' said the Sheriff. 'It will stop almost anything.'

'Almost?'

'Hold it higher.'

'Like this?'

Something caught the Sheriff's eye. 'Higher!'

A blast of heat and light hit the shield. Jack was thrown off his feet.

'Incoming!' shouted the Sheriff.

Jack landed hard on his backside with the heavy shield on top of him, but he shook his head clear.

The jack-o'-lantern was on its feet, conjuring another fireball in its pumpkin-head. The mummy had recovered too, flexing its tentacle-like bandages, whilst the scattered bones of the skeleton slowly drew together like magnets.

The Sheriff charged at the jack-o'-lantern, his sword gripped in two hands. It was the most immediate threat, due to the fireball growing in its mouth. Yet the mummy intervened, lashing at the Sheriff with its bandages. The Sheriff turned, slicing through the first batch. The mummy hissed, as though the bandages were part of its body.

But the second batch of bandages slipped through the Sheriff's defences and coiled around his limbs. The Sheriff struggled to slash at his bonds, his sword hand restricted. Meanwhile, the mummy reeled the Sheriff towards itself.

The jack-o'-lantern paid the Sheriff little attention, barging past the lion-man to renew its attack on Jack. He hastily climbed to his feet, as the demon belched another fireball. Jack ducked behind the shield, fielding the blow. This time he was ready and stayed upright. Another fireball followed. The shield was broad enough to protect Jack entirely, provided he crouched low and angled the steel disc carefully.

Come on, Jack, he told himself. *You've got this.*

The jack-o'-lantern changed tactics. Now, it unleashed a continuous jet of fire, like a flamethrower, spewing forth from its carved mouth. Once again, Jack blocked the fire with the shield and held his nerve as the flames kept on coming.

'Ow, ow, ow.'

The shield was getting hot. Of course. This was the jack-o'-lantern's intention. Heat the metal so Jack would be forced to drop it. Jack looked to the Sheriff, but the poor lion-man remained trapped in the mummy's bandages. Worse, the skeleton had fully-reformed and wielded a sword made from the bones in its right arm and hand. It looked ready to hack at the Sheriff.

Jack was on his own.

Turn to page 243.

Chapter 54

'Help!' screamed Jack. 'Please, help!'

The bear grabbed him from behind and smothered Jack's mouth with one big paw. It stifled his cries.

'That's better,' said Balam. 'Now you can watch me torture your saint. His resistance will be low because you have no faith, do you, human?'

Jack mumbled a protest into the bear's paw.

'No,' continued Balam. 'Like most of your measly race, you don't believe in anything.'

Balam turned from Jack and set his blazing eyes on Eustace. The saint met his gaze with an unwavering look of his own. Balam smirked. The hawk finally continued its attack. As before, it slowly, very slowly, began digging its talons into his scalp. Eustace's face contorted in pain, then cries of agony burst forth.

'Please, God,' mumbled Jack. 'Send more saints,

send angels, archangels, anything. Send help!'

But his plea was lost in the bear's paw once more. Even so, Jack knew in his heart that he didn't believe in Heaven and Hell, despite the two figures in front of him. He couldn't undo a lifetime of atheism after just a few hours in the company of a saint and a demon.

Eustace continued to scream. Jack hated himself for his lack of belief.

What *did* he believe in?

Joan.

Yes, he believed in his wife. He had the utmost faith in her. Strong, dependable Joan. An upstanding police officer in the community, a devoted reader, a dedicated Christian brimming with faith, and the utmost surety that it provided her in all things.

Wonderful Joan. Who always knew where the tape could be found; who could wield a whisk, a screwdriver and a baton with equal skill; who wrote poetry for her little nieces and nephews about cute little insects, with a moral to each tale; who could always find the right words to say whether she be at a wedding, baptism or funeral.

Jack may not believe in gods and devils, but he did believe in –

'Jack?'

Turn to page 286.

Chapter 55

'Answers!' he blurted.

Only one word, but it was nonsensical enough to give Balam pause for thought. The demon turned to Jack, still gripped tightly in the bear's arms.

'What did you say, human?'

'All answers,' said Jack. 'To things past, present and future. That's what Eustace said about you. That's your thing.'

'What of it?'

'Is it true?'

Eustace shook his head. 'Jack, you don't have to.'

Balam gave Jack his full attention, fiery eyes boring into him. 'I'm a Duke of Hell, human. You doubt my power?'

'I doubt everything until I see proof.'

'I've nothing to prove to a human.'

'You said yourself,' said Jack, before Balam turned back to Eustace. 'I'm a man without faith. I only believe what I see. All I'm seeing is a show of strength.'

'Careful,' warned Eustace. Balam simply glared.

Jack took a deep breath. 'Perhaps you are little more than a hodgepodge of tooth and claw. All your other powers are rumour, reputation, lies.'

Balam growled. It was a growl that came from the mouth of the bear right behind Jack. Balam marched over to Jack, bringing his snake-tail with him, and so freeing Eustace for the time being. The demon brought its intense, fiery eyes within inches of Jack's own.

'Fine, human, I'll play. You want to test me?' Balam grabbed Jack's throat. 'Ask me a question.'

Jack's mind instantly went blank.

Great plan, Jack.

'Um, what's my name?' he managed to say, despite the shaggy arms encroaching his chest, and the demon's hand around his throat.

Balam rolled his fiery eyes. 'Jack Juniper, born in Good Hope Hospital in Birmingham, England, on the twenty-third of April in the year nineteen-eighty-six.' The demon spat the words, resentful at reciting such trivial matters, but determined to prove its abilities all the same. 'Married to Joan Juniper, formerly Joan Price. No children, although you talk about it all the time. You studied English at the University of Nottingham. Now, you are employed as a website designer. You can only afford this house because the right inheritance was left to you both at the right time. You enjoy cinema, television and Halloween, though perhaps not after tonight. Your biggest fear is that your wife will leave you. Oh, and spiders. Good enough?'

Jack felt a chill down his spine. The demon knew everything. Even that thing about Joan that he had never told a soul. 'Yes, erm, that – That is all true.'

'Don't be shy, human, ask again,' said Balam, incensed by the challenge. 'Answers to everything past, present and future, remember? Ask me about the past.'

Well, this was the plan, thought Jack. *Buy as much time as possible.*

As always, when Jack was in a difficult or dangerous situation, his mind went to his strong, dependable wife.

'How did I meet my wife?' he asked.

'On Halloween,' answered Balam, without hesitation. 'At a university house party, bobbing for apples. You both bent over the barrel at the same time, bumped heads, and got talking over a shared apple. You were dressed as Batman and she was dressed as Frankenstein's monster. Is that proof enough?'

All of that *was* true. Jack didn't doubt the demon's powers. He just needed to drag this out for as long as possible to spare Eustace further torture and increase their chances of being rescued. He wished he knew the time. His wrist watch was in the house and so was Alexa.

Jack scrambled around for another question, any question.

'Wait, erm, why, why is apple-bobbing a thing?'

Turn to page 326.

Chapter 56

'I mean, yeah, somewhere, but it's pretty nasty.'

Eustace looked energised all of a sudden.

'Fetch it quickly.'

'But why?'

'Now!

'Okay!'

Jack rummaged around in his kitchen cupboards, specifically the messy ones, the dumping drawers, the ones full of batteries and cook books and chipped vases and the afternoon tea stand which they never used.

'There you are,' said Jack, retrieving a dusty dark green bottle filled with liquid the colour and viscosity of engine oil. He offered it to Eustace. 'Here. How is this going to help?'

'It'll make me stronger.'

'Dutch courage?'

'No, I don't drink before a hunt.' He smiled. 'But

you will.'

'Me?' Jack couldn't stand the stuff. He wasn't even sure why they had the bottle. Probably a leftover purchase from a stag do that was too expensive to pour down the sink. 'Why me?'

'Look at the label.'

Jack looked. It was the usual white and orange label with the stag in the middle. 'What about it?'

'See the stag?' asked Eustace. 'What do you see between its antlers?'

Jack looked closer. 'A crucifix. Wait, a crucifix? Has that always been there?'

Eustace nodded. 'It's the story of how I became a saint. I was walking through the woods and spied a beautiful deer. It would have been an easy kill, but then I saw a glowing crucifix appear between its antlers. I chose to show mercy. After that, I devoted myself to the Christian faith and I was blessed with a sainthood.'

Jack frowned. 'So, you became the patron saint of hunting by *not* hunting something?'

'The Lord moves in mysterious ways,' said Eustace, tetchily.

'I bet you've used that line before.'

'I'll be off then,' said Eustace, his hand on the door handle.

'No, no, stay!'

Eustace stayed. '*Anyway*, that bottle references my sainthood in other ways. The poem on the label, written in German, is called *Weidmannsheil* by Oskar von Riesenthal. It tells my story.'

'I know that poem,' said Jack. 'It's on the label?' Jack spotted it for the first time ever. 'Has *that* always been there?'

'Yes. Another ode to me.'

It was written on the label in German, but Jack had studied European poetry as part of a compulsory module at university. The translation of the *Weidmannsheil* poem was imprinted in his mind, having learnt it word for word for a closed-book exam. He recited it now.

> '*This is the hunter's badge of glory,*
> *That he protect and tend his quarry,*
> *Hunt with honour, as is due,*
> *And through the beast to God is true.*'

'And do you know what Jägermeister means?' asked Eustace.

'Saint Eustace Hubertus?' ventured Jack.

'Near enough. It means Hunt Master.'

Jack was baffled. 'You're saying this whole bottle of Jägermeister is a tribute to you?'

'Basically.'

'And this helps us how?'

Eustace sighed. Jack wasn't following his logic. 'If you cannot reinforce my strength with faith, then you can pay your tribute in another way.'

'What way?'

'Shots.'

'Of Jäger?' said Jack, horrified.

'Think of it as faith fuel.'

'Without a mixer? But it's horrible!'

'Much like the three things attacking your front door.' Almost on cue, there was a crash as the door buckled. 'It sounds like they've just busted through my protective seal.'

Jack hopped from one foot to the other. 'What do we do now?'

Eustace pointed at the bottle in Jack's hand.

'Chin it.'

Turn to page 255.

Chapter 57

'Hell, no,' said Jack. 'I can't stand the stuff.'

Eustace looked genuinely crestfallen. 'Never mind.'

'How would that have helped?' asked Jack.

Before Eustace could explain, there was a crash on the opposite side of the house. Jack looked to the saint in panic.

'They've broken through my protective seal,' said Eustace.

'Oh, Jesus Christ.'

'Don't swear in the name of the Lord,' chided the saint.

'Oh, motherfucking fuck.'

'That's better.'

'Is it?'

'A little less swearing and a lot more believing would give us a better advantage right now.'

'I said I was sorry,' said Jack. 'How could I have

known there was a real Heaven and Hell?'

'It's not about knowing, it's about – '

'Okay, okay,' groaned Jack. 'Point taken.' The monsters' cackling and groaning filled the house. 'So there's nothing I can do to make you more powerful? What was it you said? You're just a regular bloke with a bow?'

'Mortal, yes, but not regular.'

'How do you mean?'

Eustace slapped a hand on Jack's shoulder. 'I am one of the greatest hunters who ever lived. I am *exceptional* with this bow.'

Demonic war-cries flooded the lounge next door.

'Quickly, into the garden,' said Eustace. The saint shoved Jack through the back door. 'To the woods,' he instructed, grabbing Jack's arm and yanking him into a running pace.

'I wish I could do something to help,' panted Jack.

'Well, there is one thing.'

'Anything.'

'You're not going to like it.'

Turn to page 248.

Chapter 58

Jack leapt onto the demon's back.

His desperate attack caused the jack-o'-lantern to unleash its latest fireball in the wrong direction again. It blasted into the wall, setting it alight. The jack-o'-lantern threw Jack off, readying an attack, but now it was the Sheriff's turn to tackle the demon, bowling it over from behind. The Sheriff pinned the creature to the floor, though it continued to issue a jet of fire, igniting the carpet.

The Sheriff held the demon down but could do little else. 'Get the sword!' he shouted at Jack. 'The sword!'

Jack snatched up the sword, not knowing whether to hand over the weapon, or drive it straight through the jack-o'-lantern's head.

But he didn't have time to do either.

The skeleton reformed itself from its disparate bones. It marched towards Jack with one of its arms rearranged into a makeshift sword – an ulna lined with sharp finger bones.

Jack instinctively raised the sword to parry the skeleton's attack.

Clang!

The steel in his hands sang. Swipe after swipe followed. Jack edged away, trying his best to keep the sword raised in a defensive position.

Meanwhile, the Sheriff held onto the bucking jack-o'-lantern. He roared with fresh determination, gripped the demon's pumpkin-head in both paws and twisted violently. The pumpkin-head popped off the demon's neck. Its flames died instantly.

Meanwhile, the skeleton thrust its bone-sword at the lower-end of Jack's blade, nicking Jack's hands. It did the trick. Jack recoiled in shock, allowing the demon an opportunity to disarm him. The sword flew from his hands. The skeleton booted the defenceless Jack backwards. He landed on top of the headless mummy –

Turn to page 275.

Chapter 59

Jack snatched up the sword and drove it through the jack-o'-lantern's back with two hands on the hilt. Three feet of steel burst out of the demon's chest. It was enough to quench the fireball in its mouth.

But Jack had misjudged. The Sheriff had already started hurtling towards the jack-o'-lantern, intending to tackle the demon before it could attack. He had been mid-leap when Jack had thrust forward with the sword –

The Sheriff consequently launched himself into the blade now sticking out of the jack-o'-lantern's chest.

'Sheriff!' cried Jack.

The Sheriff roared as he drove his own midriff onto the sword, knocking the demon over. Jack barely sidestepped in time. The demon landed on its back, which meant the hilt slammed into the floor, driving the sword upwards through itself, and therefore through the Sheriff.

'Oh, shit, oh shit!'

Jack had killed his only ally in the room.

'Nobody to help you now,' said the skeleton, reforming from its scattered bones. Jack turned slowly and gulped. 'Just the two of us left.'

The skeleton pulled off its right arm, holding it forward like a rapier. The hand bones at the tip of the right arm dispersed along the arm itself, giving the edge a lethal array of sharp little finger tips.

As the skeleton attacked, Jack sorely wished he could go back and do things differently.

THE END

Chapter 60

Against all the odds, Jack managed to keep the liquid down.

'Ugh,' he murmured.

'Good, Jack,' said Eustace. 'That would have undone your tribute. My faith fuel would have been depleted.'

'Don't talk about fuel,' said Jack, still bent double, picturing the Jäger sloshing around his insides like engine oil.

The bear roared, which was a welcome distraction from his stomach. The beast began pawing the ground, getting ready to charge, with Balan grinning madly on its back.

'Now what?' he asked the saint.

'Do you happen to have a red cape?'

'No, I'm not Superman.' Turn to page 197.

'Funnily enough...' Turn to page 202.

Chapter 61

'A red cape?' repeated Jack. 'No, I'm not Superman. I'm more of a Batman guy.'

'Never mind.'

'Would that have helped?'

'Maybe.'

The bear charged at them.

'Scatter!' cried Eustace. The saint shoved Jack in one direction and ran in the other. Balam steered his bear after the saint, leaving Jack forgotten.

Then again –

He heard the flapping of wings and looked up to see Balam's hawk shooting down towards him, talons outstretched.

Jack dived to the ground, though not quickly enough. The hawk's talons tore out a tuft of his hair.

'Ow, what the hell?'

The hawk looped around for another attack. Jack sprang to his feet and sprinted to the greenhouse. It was a dilapidated structure, built from grimy glass, and filled with clutter left behind by the old couple who previously owned the house. Still, it had a door which he could put between himself and the hell-bird.

But the hawk was faster. It descended on Jack before he reached the greenhouse, scratching and clawing at his head and neck and back. Jack covered himself as best he could. He lashed outwards, realised that he still held the empty Jäger bottle. Luckily, he caught the hawk's wing with a blind swing. It was enough to knock the bird away and send it retreating to the sky.

'Not so fast.'

Jack threw the bottle at the bird, hoping to end their battle now. It missed by a mile and disappeared into the night.

'Shit.'

His attempt had only angered the bird, which soared higher in preparation for another diving attack, this time with a vengeance.

'Double shit.'

Jack bolted for the greenhouse again. He bundled

through the glass door and slammed it shut behind him.

'Good luck opening the door with talons!' he shouted madly.

Only, the bird was hurtling down towards the glass roof instead. It showed no sign of slowing, and Jack realised only a thin sheet of ancient glass was suspended between them –

Oh, I haven't thought this through.

The hawk smashed through the glass, striking Jack in the chest. He fell backwards, landing amidst neglected plant pots and half-used bags of compost. The hawk wasted no time in setting upon him with talons, beak, thrashing wings.

'Argh!'

Jack managed to grab a disused hanging basket and wedge it between himself and the hawk. The makeshift shield took the brunt of the attack, but the hawk was relentless.

There must be other things in here.

He scrambled around urgently, feeling for something sharp, a fork, a trowel, a rake – instead he found a squishy bottle with a skull on the side.

Weed killer.

Why not?

He brought the bottle upwards and squirted the hawk in the face. Again and again and again. The hawk screeched and eased its attack a little. Jack used the reprieve to roll to the side, where he found some trellis netting. He tossed the netting over the hawk. It was heavy enough to weigh the bird down, rendering its wings useless. For the moment.

Jack next spied a large ceramic plant pot. He hoisted it up with both hands, intending to trap the hawk underneath it, much like how Joan would trap spiders under a glass. But Jack fumbled the pot and it landed on the hawk with a crunch. The bird fell still.

'Ah,' said Jack, wincing. 'Sorry. No, wait. I'm not sorry. Take that, you fucking hell-bird.'

'You *will* be sorry!' roared a voice.

Balam glared at Jack on the other side of the glass door. He was still sat atop his bear. The creature swiped at the greenhouse with its mighty paws and the glass front shattered.

'Get over here, human!'

Jack did no such thing. He scurried to the far end of the greenhouse, desperately looking for a weapon, something heavy and metal. The only metal thing he found was the garden tap. It fed water into their timer-controlled sprinkler system.

Jack had an idea.

Turn to page 319.

Chapter 62

'Funnily enough, I do have a red towel. Will that help?'

'Very much. Grab it for me.'

Jack sprinted over to the clothing basket he should have brought inside earlier that evening. He rummaged through the bundle. It was damp from having been left outside. His mind wandered.

Oh, man, Joan isn't going to be happy. I'm going to have to wash this lot again.

'Hurry!' barked Eustace.

'Yes, okay, here!' He retrieved the red towel, returned to the wheelbarrow, and shoved it into the saint's hands. Eustace unfolded the towel and gripped two corners. Jack watched, bemused. 'Erm, what's the plan?'

'I'm the patron saint of Madrid, remember?'

'They like towels in Madrid?'

'They like matadors. I have spent many days at

the Plaza de Toros de Las Ventas observing the art of bull-fighting.'

'Bull-fighting?' Jack blinked. 'You know that's a bear, right?'

'Balam is one-sixth bull. Look at its left head.'

'One-sixth? Is that enough?'

'Hopefully. Once it sees red.'

'Then what?'

'I'll draw the demon away from you. Get it to charge at me instead. I can lead it to the woods where I'll have a better advantage with my bow.'

'But the back fence is on fire.'

'I believe "thank you" is the correct response.'

Before Jack could respond, the wheelbarrow was ripped up by huge paws and thrown aside.

'Come out and play, saint!' laughed Balam, atop his bear. It reared up on its hind legs.

'Run!' ordered Eustace, shoving Jack away. The demon's eyes followed Jack, until Eustace whipped the red towel about his body in a whirlwind of patterns. 'To me, Balam! Olé!'

Balam's eyes, all six pairs, focussed on the red towel. Jack watched, backing away, hoping it would work. The demon shuddered. Its central human-head drooped, face falling passive, and the fiery glow in its eyes extinguished. At the same moment, the eyes of its bull-head blazed into life instead.

And then the heads *rotated*, clicking and clacking like an ageing rollercoaster. The bull-head shifted into the central spot, whilst the human-head was relegated to the side.

'That's right, come and get me,' said Eustace, fluttering the red towel.

Balam snorted.

The bear pawed the ground, gearing up for a charge.

'Olé!' cried Eustace.

Balam charged. The bear thundered straight towards the red towel, the demon's bull instincts overriding those of his other five creatures. The saint stood fixed until the last second, then whipped the red towel aside with a twirl. Eustace narrowly avoided the creature's attack, but remained unfazed, whirling the towel about himself with flair. The demon itself charged straight past. Its momentum was too great to stop.

Jack applauded.

Eustace scowled. 'Jack, get out of here.'

Balam tugged at the bear's fur. He brought his steed around for another charge, all six pairs of eyes fixed once again on the red towel.

No, wait. Jack only counted five pairs of eyes.

Where is the hawk?

Jack glanced up in time to see outstretched talons zooming towards his head.

'Fuck!'

Turn to page 311.

Chapter 63

Jack retreated to the kitchen.

Not only was it the room furthest from the front door, it was also where he had left his phone. Every day after work, he would therapeutically decant all of the detritus from his trouser pockets – phone, keys, railcard, gum, loose change – onto the kitchen table.

There.

Jack snatched up his phone to call the police.

'Oh, you have got to be kidding me.'

He had only one percent of his battery remaining. No wonder. He had left Pokémon Go running after his walk back from the station. Nothing drained battery quite like catching 'em all. The battery lasted long enough for Jack to realise his mistake then cheerfully died in his hand. Obnoxious.

'Shit.'

Phone charger, phone charger, always on the

kitchen counter –

'But not today apparently.'

Jack dimly recalled Joan's parting words before leaving the house. Something like, 'My phone's about to die, so I'm taking the charger with me.' He had replied with the obligatory, 'Yep, okay,' keen to get her out the house.

It shouldn't have been a problem but he had left his own charger at work.

'Fuck.'

Jack and Joan had no landline phone – did anyone? – and there were no public pay phones near his house. There used to be one several roads away but that had been converted into a miniature hipster coffee outlet. Bloody gentrification.

He could go next door to ask Ivy if he could use her phone, but Ivy wouldn't answer the door on Halloween. She typically drew the curtains, turned off the lights, and went to bed early to avoid all trick-or-treaters.

Why didn't I think of that?

Jack considered getting the car out of the garage, driving away, leaving his home at the mercy of –

'Open this fucking door!' shouted a deep voice. *Uncle Finn, I presume.*

The reinforcements had arrived earlier than expected. Jack was home alone, cut off from the emergency services, with nobody to turn to for help. He swallowed hard. But something caught his eye on the kitchen counter.

Of course.

Jack wasn't alone. After all, the year was –

If your age is an even number, turn to page 79.

If your age is an odd number, turn to page 83.

Chapter 64

'Humour and wit,' croaked Jack, despite the pressure across his chest.

Balam paused and bowed his horned head with a frustrated sigh. 'Now what?'

'Eustace said you are known for your humour and wit.'

'Yes, human, what of it?'

'Does that mean you're funny?'

'I'm a hoot.'

'Okay, well, tell me a joke.'

'I'm not your jester. I'm a Duke.'

'Sounds like a touch of stage fright.'

Balam's eyes flashed dangerously. He grabbed Jack by the throat. 'You listen to me, human. I'm not frightened of anything.'

Jack struggled to breath in Balam's grip. Every word was a battle, but he had to try. 'I'm – still – not – hearing – a joke.'

Balam snarled, released Jack with a curse, and stepped away. 'Fine. How do you make holy water?'

Jack gasped, 'I don't know.'

'Boil the Hell out of it.'

Jack nodded. 'Funny. Any more?'

'Why didn't the skeleton go to the ball?'

'Tell me.'

'Because it had no body to go with.'

'Keep going.'

'Why are ghosts such bad liars?'

'Go on.'

'Because you can see right through them.'

'Another.'

'Why is Superman's costume so tight?'

'Beats me.'

'Because he wears a size S.'

'That's actually quite good. More.'

'Knock, knock.'

'Who's there?'

'Interrupting fist.'

'Interrupting fi – '

Balam slammed his fist into Jack's face. The crunch told Jack that his nose had just broken – that and the pain and the outpour of blood. He would have collapsed were it not for the bear holding him upright.

'Ow, ow, ow,' moaned Jack, head reeling from the agony.

'Hey!' shouted Eustace. 'Ignore the human, demon. Focus on me.'

'Oh, I will, saint.'

'N – no,' protested Jack, trying to focus. 'More. More jokes.'

'That's your lot, human. Now for something much more amusing. Torture.'

To scream for help, turn to page 178.

To buy more time, turn to page 212.

Chapter 65

Jack had to kill more time.

There was only one thing for it.

'What is black and white and red all over?' he blurted out.

Balam shrieked in annoyance. The bear shook Jack violently, which made his broken nose throb with fresh pain. When the bear stopped its shaking, Balam's human face was inches from Jack's own.

'I said no more jokes,' the demon roared, his eyes burning like an inferno.

Jack recoiled from the heat. He thought of his wife and found the strength to plough on. 'Not a joke. A riddle.'

'What?'

'You're renowned for your humour and wit.'

'Yes, we've been over this, human. How hard did I hit you?'

'You have proven your humour. What about wit?'

Balam glared. 'My bear is going to kill you now.'

'No, no! Then you'll never know the answer to my riddle!'

'I already know the answer!' Balam screamed in Jack's face. 'It's a newspaper!'

Jack recoiled from Balam's wrath, shutting his eyes tightly. Balam dragged out the word newspaper in a deafening shout which hurt Jack's ears and spewed the demon's rank breath all over Jack's face.

When Balam finally stopped, Jack slowly shook his head. 'No,' he said quietly. 'Not a newspaper.'

Balam seethed. 'Of course it's a newspaper.'

'Nope.'

'Oh, I see. You think you're clever, human. What dreary little answer have you got in that head of yours?'

'That would be telling.'

'An embarrassed zebra? A penguin with a rash? A tuxedo covered in ketchup? A badger in a blender? A communist nun?'

'Nope, nope, nope.'

'What then?' shrieked Balam, grabbing a fistful of Jack's hair and yanking back his head, exposing his neck. Jack trembled at the thought of Balam's snake-tail coiling up for a bite on his Adam's apple.

'A dalmatian with a nosebleed,' said Jack, surrendering.

Balam stared. He released his grip on Jack's head and tilted his head to the side, as if in thought.

WHAM.

No, not in thought. The demon was positioning one of his other heads – the ram – so it faced Jack, before using its hard, coiled horns to issue a nasty head-butt.

Fresh agony exploded in Jack's mangled nose. A new wave of hot blood poured out.

'There's your nosebleed, human,' said Balam.

Jack shook with pain. It took all his energy to stay conscious.

'Now keep your mouth shut,' warned Balam, pointing a finger in Jack's face. 'I have torturing to do. The only sound I want to hear is Eustace screaming.'

'You,' croaked Jack. 'You didn't like my riddle?'

'That wasn't a riddle. It's only a riddle if the answer is newspaper. You need the homophonic pun in order to be clever. Anything else is merely a terrible joke.'

At the risk of inviting a third blow to his nose, he goaded Balam once more.

'You think you can do better?'

Jack had to try. There was still time to kill if his plan was going to work. Admittedly, it wasn't a good plan, completely based on hope, but it was the only plan he had.

'I am Balam,' said the demon, slowly, emphasising every word. 'Demon of humour and wit. Of course, I can do better.'

'I've only heard humour so far.'

The bear growled. Balam narrowed his blazing eyes. 'I think I will kill you after all. I don't need an audience.'

The bear squeezed. Jack felt his lungs creak under the pressure.

'A wager!' he wheezed.

'What?'

The bear instantly eased its grip. Balam drew closer, intrigued. Eustace was right. Demons can never resist a wager.

'You want to bet with a demon?' asked Balam.

'If you're up to it.'

Balam grinned. His teeth were filed into points. Jack hadn't noticed that until now. He recoiled as far as he could into the bear's chest.

'What do you propose, human?'

'A game of riddles. If I win, then you let me live. If I lose, then I won't say another word.'

'No, no, no. If you lose, then you will surrender your soul to me. I will drag you to Hell where you will spend eternity as a footstall.'

Jack faltered but what choice did he have?

'Okay, deal,' he gulped.

'My *bear's* footstall,' added Balam.

'Oh.'

'Now, how many riddles? Best of three? Five?'

'Thirty-one.'

'Thirty-one?' snapped Balam.

'Today is Halloween. The thirty-first of the month. Thirty-one riddles is fitting.'

'I don't have all night, human.'

'You mean you don't have enough riddles.'

'I have thousands of riddles. Tens of thousands.

Hundreds of thousands. Thousands of – '

'Yet I'm still not hearing any.'

The bear increased the pressure again and Jack squirmed. Balam leant close. 'I'm going to enjoy enslaving you for eternity.' Jack's mouth went dry. 'If you want a game of riddles, then so be it. Enjoy your last ever moments above ground.'

'Jack,' shouted Eustace. 'Take it back. You don't have to do this. Not for me.'

Balam scowled in frustration, stomped over to Eustace and kicked the saint in the face. It was enough to knock him unconscious. His halo winked out, like a broken bulb.

'Now,' said Balam. 'Where was I? Ah, yes. Here is your first riddle.'

'Why do you get to ask first?'

'Because I say so. And my bear is one hug away from crushing the life out of you.'

Jack sighed. 'Fair enough.'

'Let's begin.'

Turn to page 293.

Chapter 66

No, Jack, no. You have to think straight.

He had to ignore the kids, tempting though it was to swing the door open and scream at them to fuck off, *fuck off, FUCK OFF.*

It wasn't worth being caught red-handed, literally, and being sent to prison. Not because of some obnoxious trick-or-treaters.

Ding dong.

Instead, he ploughed on with a frustrated growl, scrubbing, scrubbing, scrubbing. He took deep breaths, reining in his panic, and focussed on the positives. Joan had gotten what she deserved for breaking his heart in such a vicious manner. Now, he had complete freedom for the rest of his life. No more heartbreak, no more nagging – this entire house was his alone and he could enjoy that solitude forever.

Ding dong.

The trick-or-treaters could wear themselves out on his doorbell. He was one clean floor away from being free of Joan for the rest of his life.

A new sound.

'Huh?'

It sounded like someone trying his front door handle. Surely, the trick-or-treaters wouldn't be reckless enough, or so horny for sugar, that they would let themselves into his house?

But now there was a second new sound. His front door was creaking open. A door which he hadn't thought to lock, apparently.

'Cheeky little bastards,' he said, hurriedly tidying up.

There was no third sound, which he found the most troubling of all. Jack expected to hear the voice of a parent immediately snapping at their kids for touching his front door handle, or at least the call of a pushy child saying, 'Hellooo? Trick or treat?'

Jack froze, listening, heart beating. He was in a difficult position. He couldn't chase them off without them seeing him covered in blood and thereby incriminating himself.

'Who's there?' he barked in the meanest voice he could muster. Hopefully that would be enough. But just to be sure, 'Get out of my house!'

Still no reply but there were now footsteps in the lounge, shuffling towards the kitchen door.

'I said get out!'

More footsteps.

Fuck, fuck.

Only one thing for it. He really didn't want to, but what choice did he have?

Jack snatched up his trusty murder weapon and stood ready on his side of the kitchen door. It slowly opened to reveal –

'Joan?'

He dropped the knife and collapsed, landing hard on his knees.

'Happy Halloween, Jack,' said the ghost of Joan, with a triumphant grin. She towered over him. 'You picked a bad night to kill me.'

Of course. Halloween. This was supposedly the time of year when the fabric of the world grew thin and creatures could pass through from the other side. If only he had waited one more day.

'Joan,' he croaked. 'What do you want? Are you going to kill me?'

'No, I'm a ghost.' She passed an ethereal arm through his head. It held no more substance than mist. Jack felt nothing except a slight chill. 'I can't harm you.' Jack must have looked relieved because she was quick to add, 'Not physically at least.'

'What do you mean?'

'I think I will hang around here. This is my house, after all. I can't stab you with a kitchen knife but I can butcher your mind. Would you like to know more about my liaisons with Ted? Would you like to hear every sordid detail?'

'No, please, I don't want to hear it.'

'I can talk you through our encounters, all of them, every second of every day, describing each filthy act, over and over and over.'

'No, no, no.'

'I will never stop. I don't eat, I don't sleep –'

'No!'

'And as you know, I can talk forever.'

THE END

Chapter 67

The three monsters seethed, angrier than ever. The jack-o'-lantern belched fire through its carved mouth. Several of the mummy's bandages came loose, rising up like snakes to a charmer's tune, each a cobra poised to strike. The skeleton spread all ten fingers in front of itself. Each fingertip was filed into a sharp point, all directed at Jack like ten darts ready to fly.

Jack closed his eyes and thought of Joan.

But –

The next sound he heard was a curious one, like somebody had emptied a bucket of sand on his doorstep. Curiosity compelled him to open one eye, then the other.

'Huh?'

The jack-o'-lantern was gone. In its place sat a pile of sand.

No, not sand, he realised. *Sawdust*.

The skeleton and mummy stared in confusion then looked at Jack with the utmost vitriol. They didn't even say the word trick this time, but Jack knew they were thinking it. The mummy's bandages prepared to attack but then they turned to dust too, disintegrating one by one, followed by the mummy itself.

The skeleton, now flanked by its henchmen's ashes, looked ready to scream at Jack, in what would surely have been a war-cry befitting a banshee.

But its jaw poured away into sawdust before it could utter a sound. The skull caved in on itself next, followed by the rest of its bones. Even the black robe turned to powder. The whole process took a matter of seconds. All that remained was the jaunty top hat, sat atop the pile of sawdust.

'I guess those weight loss bars *do* work,' said Jack, bewildered.

He then recalled the monsters had revived from their other treat-induced ailments, so Jack wasted no time in kicking each pile of sawdust as hard as he could. The autumn evening wind caught the dust and carried much of it away.

Jack had no intention of letting the monsters rematerialise, so he retrieved a broomstick from the garage and madly brushed the remaining dust as thinly as possible, in as many directions as possible. When he was satisfied that the piles were suitably diminished, he leant on his broomstick, exhausted.

The top hat remained. Jack couldn't help himself. He picked it up – quick check, nothing weird inside – and placed it on his head.

'Spoils of war,' he said.

Jack then sat on his front garden wall, broomstick resting across his lap, in case the wind brought the monsters back.

Turn to page 323.

Chapter 68

Wait, the bottle!

The empty Jäger bottle had missed the hell-bird when Jack had thrown it earlier, but it now lay on the grass, within reach. He snatched it up, desperately.

Jack didn't know any prayers or blessings, but he did know the Weidmannsheil poem on the Jäger label. He shouted the words as he fled from the hawk, running in circles, ducking and diving, but never lessening his grip on the bottle, and never once stopping his recital:

> *'This is the hunter's badge of glory,*
> *That he protect and tend his quarry.'*

The bottle started to glow in his hand. It surprised him at first and he almost dropped it, but he recognised the glow as the same bright, white light that shone from Eustace's halo.

> *'Hunt with honour, as is due,*
> *And through the beast to God is true.'*

The bottle was warm to the touch by the end of his recital. Jack hadn't known what would happen when he started the poem, but he hoped *something* would happen. A glowing bottle of Jägermeister was definitely something.

Jack stopped, turned, and swiped at the attacking hawk. It was a direct hit. The hawk obliterated the moment the bottle made contact, leaving a blitz of feathers and sparkling dust. Balam's other five selves – man, bear, bull, ram, snake – felt the loss. They recoiled as though struck themselves. The three-headed Balam leered at Jack, marching towards him through the excruciating patter of holy water.

Jack was ready. He launched the glowing bottle as hard as he could. It sailed through the air like a comet and smashed on Balam's middle head.

Balam crumpled instantly, dropping to the ground, unconscious. The bear passed out too, it being only an extension of the same demon. They weren't getting up. The water from the sprinklers finished them off, leaving behind two big puddles.

Jack stared.

'We won?'

Saint Eustace appeared at his shoulder, drenched, heavily-wounded after being mauled by the bear. 'Looks that way.'

'Did I just – bottle a demon?' asked Jack.

'You saved my life.'

'By bottling a demon.'

'Yes.'

'With a bottle.'

Eustace shrugged. 'Not every warrior wields a sword. Not every hunter carries a bow.'

Jack was still grasping the situation. 'We defeated a Duke of Hell with a sprinkler system and an empty bottle of Jäger.'

'No.' Eustace patted Jack on the shoulder. 'We defeated a Duke of Hell with words and belief. Much more powerful weapons than anything found in an armoury.'

'Words and belief,' repeated Jack to himself.

'I need to go,' said Eustace, indicating the bear wounds on his torso. He was soaking in blood. Jack could see bone and vital organs.

Jack gasped. 'Shit, Eustace. I'll call you an ambulance.'

'No need.' He looked to the sky and shouted, 'Metatron, send a stairway!'

As requested, an ornate, metal staircase spiralled down from the stars and slammed into the ground beside them.

'What the – ' Jack jumped aside.

'Stairway to Heaven,' explained Eustace, stepping onto the first step.

Jack considered the metal railings which ran up the stairway. They were intricately designed, incorporating the shape of a deer's head.

'Can I come with you?' said Jack. 'Take a look?'

'Better not.' Eustace sank down onto the steps, clutching the railing tightly in one hand, and holding his ruined stomach with the other. 'It's not a place for the living.'

'Oh.'

'Your place is here.'

Jack looked around. The Balam puddle was seeping into the grass, disappearing.

'Should I worry about that?' he asked. 'Am I going to have demonic flowers sprouting in the Spring? Sinflowers? Dantelions?' Jack laughed at his puns, a little too loudly, and a little too high in pitch.

'I think you need some rest,' observed Eustace.

'I think – you're right.'

'Remember, Jack. Words and belief.'

'My wife's two favourite hobbies.'

'Smart lady. Goodbye, Jack.'

The stairway ascended into the sky. Jack watched for a while, then a thought struck him.

'How am I going to explain this to Joan?' he called after the departing saint.

There was just enough time for Eustace to give his reply before disappearing into the stars above.

'Words.'

Jack nodded to himself.

And belief.

THE END

Chapter 69

'Alexa,' he rasped, unable to look away from the poised finger, ready to plunge. 'Play hymns.'

The skeleton startled at the word, its drawn arm suddenly wilting.

'Hymn?' it said. The other two looked at each other. The monsters recognised the word. They slowly turned to the smart speaker, watching its blue corona of light turning around and around, processing the request.

'Playing selected hymn mix on Spotify.'

The sweet music began.

Jack didn't recognise the song, or even the language in which it was sung, but it was powerful, operatic and beautiful, and clearly divine because the effect it had on the monsters was instantaneous. They jerked their heads left and right, making upset noises, much like humans do when a bumblebee hovers in front of their face.

'Alexa,' rasped Jack, despite the skeleton's grip on his throat. 'Turn it up to eleven.'

BOOM.

The hymn music erupted from the smart speaker in crystal-clear sound. The monsters slapped their hands over their ears. They writhed and hissed in pain. The fire inside the jack-o'-lantern extinguished. The carved pumpkin rolled off its shoulders to the ground, leaving nothing but a headless robe.

The mummy collapsed next. The bandages binding Jack's hands and neck drooped away, along with the bandages which wrapped the mummy itself. Evidently, the bandages were the only thing holding the mummy's rotting green body together. Once they had unravelled, the zombie underneath fell apart in moist clumps.

That only left the skeleton. It clutched the sides of its head, despite not having ears. Its skull split vertically down the middle with a sickening crack, though the monster wasn't going down without a fight. It swiped at Jack with its sharp fingers. Thankfully, now Jack was free of the mummy's bandages, he could recoil quickly enough to avoid his face being slashed to ribbons.

The skeleton didn't manage a second swipe. Its arm fell off at the socket, then the rest of its bones lost whatever dark hex had been holding them upright. The power of the hymn had torn through that hex. The skeleton's bones clattered noisily to the floor. Its skull followed, striking the kitchen tiles and shattering into pieces.

Jack stared at all three mounds of monster for quite some time before he had the strength to climb to his feet.

'Alexa,' he said. 'Stop.'

The beautiful hymn cut off immediately. The kitchen delved into an eerie silence. He kept expecting to hear a ghostly whisper demanding sugar. Eventually, it grew so quiet that he couldn't stand it.

'Alexa, say something.'

'What would you like me to say?'

'Anything.'

'Would you like a joke?'

'Anything.'

'Why didn't the skeleton go to the ball?'

'Not that.'

THE END

Chapter 70

'Finished downloading Ordained Skill,' said Alexa. *'Would you like me to perform a marriage ceremony?'*

'Not today, thanks,' said Jack in a raspy voice. The mummy's bandage constricted his throat. 'Alexa, bless the water in the sprinklers.'

Sprinkler systems were fitted in new build homes as standard following the increase in home and apartment block fires that arose in the late teenies and early twenties.

'Blessing,' confirmed Alexa.

'Bless?' said the skeleton, looking around urgently. It knew the word, maybe even feared it. The jack-o'-lantern didn't even hesitate, too preoccupied brewing up a fireball to melt Jack's face. The flames inside its head were white-hot now. Jack could already feel his skin scorching.

'Blessing complete.'

The mummy's bandage tightened around Jack's

throat, but he gargled with all his might and main.
'Alexa, turn on the sprinklers!'

The jack-o'-lantern opened its mouth –

'Turning on sprinklers.'

And the sprinklers burst into life.

The deluge was instant, drenching the kitchen with water within seconds. Only, this was holy water, blessed by the freshly-ordained Alexa, and the monsters howled in agony. The jack-o'-lantern's flames were doused by rivulets of water pouring through its triangular eye-holes. Meanwhile, the pumpkin-head itself sizzled and steamed, as though it were being showered with acid, rather than tepid water.

The other two were in equal torment. The water burned through the mummy's bandages, each droplet forming a hole in the material, until the bandages were so pockmarked that they fell apart entirely. The mummy itself followed suit. Evidently, it had only been held together by its bandages, so it soon collapsed into a bubbling pile of green putty.

As for the skeleton, its jaunty top hat went awry as its skull melted in on itself. Its whole body lost rigidity, as though it were made of plasticine, not bone, and it flopped to the floor like an empty wet suit.

The jack-o'-lantern was the last demon standing. Its body eroded under the barrage of water. The pumpkin-head tumbled all the way down to the kitchen tiles, where it burst open like a rotten tomato.

The kitchen reached a state of relative calm, once the monsters had stopped screaming in pain. Their remains simmered in the water, turning to mush, then dissolving. The only sound that remained was the patter of water teeming down from the ceiling.

'Alexa, stop the sprinklers.'

'Stopping sprinklers.'

The water ceased.

Jack's leg remained punctured by the skeleton's sharp fingers, buried deep in his flesh like shrapnel. But he noticed that a thin trickle of steam was rising from each entry wound. He realised the fingers would dissolve like the rest of the skeleton. He scooped up handfuls of holy water from the floor to speed up the process. Next, he would have to treat the wounds, drain the kitchen, and fix the front door, all before Joan came home.

All this chaos over a little –

'Alexa,' said Jack, before he forgot. 'Add sugar to the shopping list.'

THE END

Chapter 71

'Sheriff?' Jack repeated. He looked down at the book in his hands, sporting a lion on the cover, then back up at the lion in his study. 'You're the Sheriff?'

'One of them, yes. If you didn't bring me here, then – '

The monstrous sounds of the demons could be heard through the floorboards. There was smashing and crashing and the manic giggles of the jack-o'-lantern.

'What is happening down there?' asked the Sheriff.

'I'm under attack,' said Jack. 'Three demons have broken into my home.' He gulped. 'I think they want to eat me.'

'Why?'

'Because I'm full of sugar.'

The Sheriff fixed Jack with a stare, as though trying to decide whether Jack was a liar or just plain crazy, but whatever face Jack pulled seemed to convince the Sheriff that he was telling the truth.

'Very well. The mystery of my arrival can wait. Let us address your demon problem first.'

'You'll help me?' said Jack, delirious with relief.

'Of course. I am one of the twelve Sheriffs, sworn to uphold the Two Rules of Nephos.'

'The Two Rules?'

'The second rule is to keep the peace.' There was a timely crash downstairs, followed by violent thudding and the shattering of glass. Cackling laughter followed. 'It sounds like these demons haven't come in peace. It is time I had a word with them.'

'Thank you, Sheriff.' Jack paused. 'Wait, what's the first rule?'

The Sheriff looked uneasy. 'No going back to Earth.'

'Ah.'

'Evidently I have broken one of the rules I have sworn to uphold.' He shook his mane. 'But it can wait. Let's meet these demons of yours.'

'They're terrifying,' said Jack. 'Better draw your

sword.'

'Not yet,' said the Sheriff. 'I have been wrong about demons before. They don't always mean you harm. Sometimes they are simply misunderstood.'

'These ones definitely mean me harm.'

'Are you sure?'

The floor gave way beneath them. The Sheriff and Jack dropped into the lounge below, books landing around them with thuds and flops. Flames licked the walls around them, whilst the three monsters lined up, each in a battle stance.

'Pretty sure!' yelled Jack, having landed painfully on his back.

'Point taken,' said the Sheriff. He had landed on all fours with leonine grace. He stood up to his full height to address the demons. 'Who are you and what do you want with this man?'

'Now, now,' said the skeleton. 'Curiosity killed the cat.'

The mummy gave a low laugh. The jack-o'-lantern tittered away.

'I'm not a cat,' said the Sheriff.

'Lion then. Close enough.'

'I'm not a lion.'

'Freak then.'

'Freak,' muttered Jack. 'That's rich, coming from a talking skeleton.'

'I'm not a freak either,' said the Sheriff, steadily.

'Then what are you?' snapped the skeleton.

The Sheriff stepped forwards, unslinging his shield and drawing his sword.

'Bored of this conversation.'

The Sheriff flung his shield at the skeleton. It flew like a large metal discus, catching the skeleton in the ribcage and knocking its bones all asunder. At the same time, the Sheriff flicked his sword in a way that caused the sheath to fly from the end like a javelin. The sheath speared the mummy through its rotten midriff. The creature fell back in surprise.

Finally, the Sheriff booted Jack and Joan's innate footstall at the jack-o'-lantern. Jack had complained when Joan had added the footstall to their IKEA trolley, saying it was unnecessary. Sure enough, they had barely given it a second glance in the years since. But as the footstall sailed towards the jack-o'-lantern and hit it squarely in its big pumpkin-head,

Jack was very thankful indeed for its existence indeed.

'You did it!' cried Jack, scrambling to his feet.

The Sheriff shook its head. 'It will take more than that, I fear.'

'It will?'

'Fight by my side.'

'I'm sorry?'

'Which do you want? Sword or shield?'

To accept the sword, turn to page 171.

To accept the shield, turn to page 175.

Chapter 72

'Screw it.'

Jack charged forward, with the shield raised, running towards the jet of flame. His adrenaline had kicked in, along with all the sugar he had consumed earlier that evening. Besides, the demons were small, almost child-sized. Perhaps they were just a trio of teenage monsters, broken free from Hell to look for mischief.

Just?

Jack drove the shield forward until he reached the jack-o'-lantern, then shoved the shield into its face. It had the desired effect. The demon was stunned enough to stop belching flame. The hacking noise prompted by the impact suggested it was choking on its own flames. No time to stop. Jack shoved the shield into the demon again and again.

Smack, smack, smack.

The demon hissed every time. Jack realised that

the metal must be red-hot on the front side of the shield. For a creature capable of conjuring fire inside its head, it was surprisingly sensitive to heat on the outside. Its orange skin sizzled. Jack wasted no time in pressing the shield against its face. The creature howled in pain. It ran for the door.

But before Jack could celebrate –

Oh shit, the Sheriff.

The bad news: the Sheriff was still bound by the mummy's bandages. The good news: the skeleton had stopped advancing on the Sheriff with its bone-sword. The worse news: the skeleton was now coming for Jack.

Oh shit, me!

It swiped its bone-sword at Jack, who instinctively met the blow with the shield. More blows followed.

Clang, clang, clang.

The skeleton was too fast with its attack. Jack was soon overwhelmed and stumbled on something whilst backing away. It was enough of a distraction for the skeleton to hook its bone-sword on the edge of the shield, yanking it from Jack's hands.

Jack was now unarmed and undefended, crawling backwards, eyes staring up in fear at the advancing skeleton. The demon raised its bone-sword high –

And stepped in something.

The skeleton immediately sank downwards, all the way to its left thigh, as though it had stepped into an open manhole. Instead, it had stepped into an open copy of *The Sheriff*. Faint whispers of smoke curled from its pages.

No, not smoke. Cloud.

This was the Sheriff's way home. He had arrived through the bookcase. He would return through the book. It made as much sense as anything else right now.

The skeleton struggled. It couldn't lift itself out of the book with only one arm, so it shoved its bone-sword back into its empty socket. The bones quickly reformed into an arm once again. Then it put both hands on the carpet and pushed itself upwards.

Meanwhile –

Over the skeleton's shoulder, Jack watched the bound Sheriff try a new tactic. Instead of trying to break free of the mummy's bandages, he grabbed them tightly with his paws. The Sheriff grinned, finally realising that *he* wasn't tied to the *mummy* – the *mummy* was tied to *him*.

He pulled.

The mummy stumbled forward and stepped on the discarded, red-hot shield. The dry bandages on its foot burst into flame. They quickly spread up its body. The demon howled.

The Sheriff took advantage of the mummy's predicament, yanking on the bandages once again. This time, the mummy flew forward and met the Sheriff's fist, which punched right through its crusty, zombie head. The bandages dropped off the Sheriff in an instant. The Sheriff now had full freedom of movement to whirl the burning, headless mummy around the lounge on its bandages, like an athlete participating in a hammer throw –

And threw its body into the skeleton.

The impact was enough to shatter the skeleton like a set of skittles. Bones flew everywhere. The Sheriff let go of the bandage and the projectile mummy crashed into the TV cabinet. It crumpled into a smouldering, crackling pile.

Jack and the Sheriff joined each other in the middle of the lounge, breathing heavily.

'Two down,' said the Sheriff. 'Where did the jack-o'-lantern go?'

'Wait, look,' said Jack.

Turn to page 266.

Chapter 73

'Happy Halloween to me,' said Jack, miserably.

Saint Eustace Hubertus had tied Jack up and left him alone in a leafy clearing, deep in the woods beyond the top of his garden. A dark line of trees surrounded him. This was his role.

Bait.

Eustace was out there in the thick wooded trees, lying in wait somewhere, ready for the demons.

'Eustace, please,' called Jack. 'Is this really necessary?'

No response from the saint. Not even a shush. Naturally, the greatest hunter who ever lived wasn't going to simply give his position away by making a noise.

Snap.

Nor was Eustace likely to make the amateur mistake of stepping on a twig. The demons approached.

Jack had watched Eustace set his traps before vanishing into the trees, but that didn't make him feel any better about the demons.

Snap.

Jack didn't have Eustace's uncanny ability to see in the dark, and the moonlight seeping through the canopy overhead was sparse, yet even Jack could make out the fiery triangles of the jack-o'-lantern's eyes in the trees ahead.

They're here.

It was the skeleton who attacked first. The demon hurtled forth from the trees, sharp fingers swinging by its sides.

It was a short-lived hurtle. The skeleton ran into Eustace's first trap, a thin trip wire strung up at shin height. The skeleton tripped and fell to the ground, face-first. An arrow flew from the woods, flying directly towards the skeleton's exposed back –

Only, it was a skeleton, after all. The arrow passed harmlessly through its hollow ribcage and out the other side. The skeleton cackled, delighted, rising to its feet. It pointed a bony finger at the spot of trees from where the arrow had emerged.

'There!'

The jack-o'-lantern stepped into the clearing and belched a stream of flames at the trees in question. They caught instantly, blazing into a hot white-orange-red inferno. This continued for some time, then the jack-o'-lantern finally stopped to catch its breath. Its pumpkin-head grinned, victorious. The demons had anticipated the trap. Their enemy would surely be a bundle of charred bones by now.

Then again –

An arrow flew from the trees on the *opposite* side of the clearing. It sailed through the air and stuck in the back of the jack-o'-lantern's pumpkin-head. The demon stood for a moment, still dumbly starring in the wrong direction at its fiery handiwork, then flopped face-down on the wet leaves.

'What?' snapped the skeleton.

The first arrow had been triggered by the trip-wire, not fired by Eustace's own hand. As if the patron saint of hunting would miss, even when aiming at a creature without flesh.

But Eustace did need time to draw another arrow. The closely-packed woods meant that it took the saint longer than usual. All of which gave the skeleton time to find its feet and charge at Jack.

'I'll rip you apart!' it promised.

Although, the last word was cut short. The ground rose up around the skeleton, yanking it into the air. The hunter's net had worked, concealed under fallen leaves until triggered by the skeleton's weight. The demon thrashed wildly in its trappings, screaming all manner of threats. An arrow whistled through the air. It found a home deep within the netted bundle of bones, dirt and leaves.

The demon fell silent.

'Two down,' said Jack, heart pounding. 'Where's my mummy?'

Jack scanned the lines of trees in front of him, striving to see any movement in the woods. He imagined Eustace doing the same. He stretched his neck in all directions. Where was the damn thing?

He felt a musty breath on top of his head.

Um?

Turn to page 306.

Chapter 74

The Sheriff offered Jack a paw and pulled him to his feet.

'Are you hurt?' asked the Sheriff.

'Just mentally and psychologically.'

'Good enough.'

'I threw the skull into your world.'

'Quick thinking.' The Sheriff considered the open book, churning out cloud vapour. 'This is my way back to Nephos? Through a book?'

'Looks that way.'

'Curious.'

'The skull is on that side.'

'I'll boot it from the edge of a cloud. Let it tumble into the Undercurrent. Play it safe.'

Jack didn't understand but he nodded all the same. 'And I'll burn these bodies.'

'Good.'

The cloud vapour churned more eagerly from the

pages now, inviting the Sheriff to return to his world, to his reality.

'Well fought, Jack,' said the Sheriff, extending his paw.

'And you, Sheriff.'

I'm shaking a lion's paw, thought Jack. *What an evening.*

The Sheriff went to step into the open book, but he paused. 'I have to ask, what book is this?'

Jack hesitated. The Sheriff didn't know he was a character in a fantasy series. That sort of thing couldn't be good to hear.

'Best not to ask questions,' said Jack. 'Too many answers can make a person crazy.'

'Agreed. Although there is one answer that I must have.'

'Go on.'

'Why *didn't* the skeleton go to the ball?'

Jack grinned. 'Because it had no body to go with.'

The Sheriff stared for a moment, then bared its sharp teeth. Jack took a step back before realising it was a smile. 'Ah, a joke. Very good. Farewell, Jack.'

The Sheriff jumped into the book with both feet,

dropping through the mass of cloud. Gone in the blink of an eye. Jack was tempted to follow, but curiosity killed the cat, as the skeleton had said. In any case, the unfurling cloud had ceased. It now withdrew into the pages, until the last wisp disappeared and only the open book remained.

'Farewell, Sheriff.'

Jack picked up the book and flicked through the pages. It was no longer a magical portal, merely Joan's well-thumbed copy of her favourite book.

Jack had bodies to burn and a whopping great hole in his lounge ceiling, but he also had to know more about his savior and the world from whence he came. Jack sank into his sofa and turned to the first page.

THE END

Chapter 75

'Come on, to the woods,' called Eustace, moments later, as they sprinted up Jack's long back garden. There was a woodland stretching beyond the fence at the very top of his garden.

'Why the woods?' panted Jack, between forced swigs of Jäger.

'I'm a hunter, not a warrior. Most lethal when moving amongst the trees.'

They almost made it to the fence when a fireball flew between them and blasted the wooden gate they had been headed towards. Jack and Eustace skidded to a halt and turned to see the three demons scurrying up the garden after them. The fence burned hot on their backs.

'Nowhere left to run,' said Jack.

'Maybe I will have to be a warrior, after all,' said Eustace. 'How is that Jäger going down?'

'Slowly,' said Jack, forcing another swig. 'But

almost gone.'

'Good, I'll need it. Drink up. Faith fuel, remember?'

Jack nodded reluctantly and knocked back even more. Meanwhile, Eustace drew three arrows on his bow string, eyes narrowed at the approaching demons, just twenty feet away and closing. The saint whispered something under his breath – a prayer, surely? – and let all three arrows fly at once.

The arrows fanned outwards as they flew through the air, setting aflame whilst in flight. The flames were bright and white, giving off a holy starlight. The three demons stared dumbstruck as the arrows found a home in each of their heads. Moments later, their heads caught alight, burning with the same intensity as the arrows.

'Are they – are they pulling off their own heads?' asked Jack.

They were.

The demons writhed in alarm, hands clamped on either side of their burning heads, tugging, struggling –

The jack-o'-lantern was first, breaking its pulpy

pumpkin-head in two. Orange flesh and pumpkin seeds the size of fingernails showered the grass. Beneath the pumpkin was another head.

'They were masks, after all,' said Jack to himself.

Unexpectedly, it was an animal's head.

'Wait, a bull?'

Jack turned to Eustace who stared in shock. The saint hadn't even reloaded his bow.

'Eustace?'

The mummy's burning head fell apart next, crumbling away, to reveal –

'Is that a sheep?' asked Jack, staring.

'A ram.' Eustace had gone pale.

'Close enough.'

'I wish.' The saint took a step back.

Finally, the skeleton's skull cracked in two, neatly splitting in half like an egg.

'Now what?' asked Jack. 'A cow? A chicken?'

'No, a man,' predicted Eustace. 'With burning red eyes.'

Sure enough, when the skull fell away, it revealed the face of a gaunt, pale man with fiery eyes. The man leered at them with an unpleasant grin.

'How did you know it would be a man?'

'He's an old enemy.'

'And the other two? The bull and ram?'

'The same enemy.'

The three demons – man, bull and ram – touched their heads together, with the red-eyed man in the middle. The contact triggered a spell. All three of their bodies shimmered and transformed into a rippling, black substance like an oil slick. The bodies then lost their shape and glooped together to form one large, bubbling blob, which started to expand outwards into something much bigger. Jack thought he could see ancient symbols, not unlike hieroglyphics, darting over the black surface of the blob like a shoal of fish.

'What is happening?' asked Jack, transfixed.

'Get down.' Eustace shoved Jack to the ground behind an upturned wheelbarrow.

'Eustace, what is that thing?'

The saint swallowed hard. 'His name is Balam.'

Turn to page 279.

Chapter 76

Coolness. Starlight. Silence.

A horse?

Jack dropped onto a white, spongey material, not unlike snow. The Sheriff was beside him once again, along with an enormous horse.

'What happened?' asked the Sheriff. 'This is Nephos. How did you get us back?'

'I saw a b – ' It was probably best not to mention that the Sheriff was a fictional character in a bestselling book. 'I saw a window, an opening. It looked like a way out. A way back.'

'Did you shut the window behind you?'

'Erm.'

Jack looked around. There was no copy of *The Sheriff* on this side. No swirling portal above their heads. It looked like a one-way trip.

The Sheriff readied his sword. 'The demons will follow us.'

'I don't think they will,' said Jack. 'The room was on the verge of collapse.'

Although I've been wrong before.

The Sheriff waited a few moments to be sure, Jack's heart pounding all the while, then breathed a heavy sigh. 'Very well,' he said, shouldering his shield and sheathing his sword. 'It has been an odd night.'

I know the feeling, thought Jack. *I jumped into my wife's favourite book.*

They stood close to the edge of the cloud, with a vast starscape above them, and a glimpse of Earth below, lit up like a Christmas tree. The cloud itself was featureless, apart from the odd, scrawny tree.

The horse whinnied. It was tall, dark grey in colour, and loaded with a heavy travel-pack. Jack thought its whinny carried a tone. Part-reproachful, part-bewildered.

'Sorry, Pal,' said the Sheriff, scratching her steed's ears. 'I didn't mean to leave you on your own. Trust me, you were better off here.'

'This is your horse?'

'Sky-horse,' corrected the Sheriff. 'Palladium,

Jack. Jack, Palladium.'

'What can a sky-horse do?'

The Sheriff had no time to answer. The skeleton dropped out of the sky, wielding its fey arm-bone sword again, only now its bones were charred black and radiating heat.

It uttered a ghastly war-cry, sprinting straight for Jack –

– then shattered into a hundred pieces. The sky-horse had hoofed the demon with both hind legs.

Ouch.

'*That* is what a sky-horse can do,' confirmed the Sheriff. He picked up the skeleton's skull before the demon could reform and bowled it over the edge of the cloud. It plummeted into the nothingness below. As Jack watched the skull vanish from view, he liked to think the skull had finally stopped grinning.

The sky-horse, Palladium, stomped the skeleton's remaining bones into dust.

'Good riddance,' said the Sheriff.

'But how do I get back?' asked Jack. On the other side, the book had surely been burnt to cinders by now.

'I don't know,' said the Sheriff. 'We can ask the Maverick.'

'The who?'

'The Maverick.' The Sheriff indicated the M emblazoned on his shield. 'He rules over the clouds.'

Jack suddenly regretted not having read the Nephos books. It would have come in handy now that he was living in them.

'I don't know anything about this world.'

'We have a long journey to the Wind Chime,' said the Sheriff, looking East. 'I will answer all of your questions.'

'Okay, tell me everything. Start from the beginning.'

'Very well. In the beginning, there was the Clown and He was sad.'

THE END

Chapter 77

The saint was tall and barrel-chested with a bald head. He looked more like a bouncer than a loyal servant of God. His skin was weathered and worn, as though he had spent more time outside than under a roof. He was dressed in dark browns and greens, with leather gloves on each hand and sturdy boots to match. Slung over his broad back was a backpack, a quiver and an enormous bow, which would have drawn Jack's eye, had it not been for the glowing halo hovering above the man's head.

'Where are the monsters?' asked Jack.

'I managed to drive them outside,' said Eustace. 'They didn't expect to see a saint. I think I spooked them, but they won't scare so easily a second time.'

'The door won't keep them out.'

'It will for a while. I scratched a cross onto the door before I wedged it shut. The demons will be stung if they touch the wood, but not for long.'

'What do we do?'

'Head to the garden.'

'The garden?'

'Follow me. Quickly.'

'Eustace, what are you the patron saint of, exactly?'

'Hunting, mostly.' Eustace tapped the bow on his back. 'Also, mathematicians, metalworkers, trappers, firefighters, torture victims, and the city of Madrid.'

'Madrid?'

'Oh, and opticians.'

'Opticians?' Jack stared. 'Anything else?'

'Nope, that's everything.' He counted on his fingers. 'Mathematicians, metalworkers, trappers, firefighters, torture victims, the city of Madrid, and opticians, but mostly hunting.' He gripped Jack's shoulder. 'Now let's hunt some demons.'

Eustace sped down the stairs. Jack followed.

'Why are we going to the garden?' he asked. 'Shouldn't we barricade ourselves inside?'

'You said it yourself,' replied the saint. 'Doors won't keep the demons out.'

'But the garden?'

'Your garden backs onto a wooded area,' explained Eustace, as they cut through the lounge. 'Woods are where I do my best work. I'm a hunter, not a warrior. I can defeat the demons, but only on my turf.'

'Shall I stay here?' said Jack, as they reached the kitchen. 'Hide in a closet?'

'They're after you, not me,' said Eustace.

'Oh.'

'They'll smell the sugar in your blood. Sniff you out.'

'Ah.'

'Probably best to stick by my side.'

Eustace stopped and turned when they reached the door to the back garden.

'What is it?' asked Jack. 'Are they out there?'

'No, I need to ask you something before we go outside,' said Eustace, gravely. 'You have to tell me the truth. It could be a matter of life or death.'

'Yes, okay, anything.'

'Do you believe in God?'

Turn to page 168.

Chapter 79

'The skeleton is reforming,' said Jack.

'Already?' said the Sheriff.

The Sheriff grabbed the skeleton's skull from the carpet before it could be drawn back onto its neck. Perhaps, he planned to smash the skull to pieces, but the skeleton's headless body was too quick in its reassembly. It launched an immediate attack on the Sheriff, bone-sword back in hand.

'Here, hold this!' said the Sheriff, tossing the skull to Jack, so his hands were free for his sword.

Jack caught it by surprise.

'Whoa!'

He nearly lost the skull just as quickly because it tried to fly from his hands to re-join its body. Instead, Jack held the skull tightly, hugging it to his body. The skull didn't like that.

'Ow!'

The skull bit him. Jack renegotiated his grip,

holding it higher, his thumbs through each eye socket, as far away from the snapping teeth as he could manage.

Still, it didn't stop the skull pushing forward, gnashing, trying to get a grip on Jack's throat –

BANG.

The lounge door slammed open. The jack-o'-lantern returned. Its pumpkin-head was charred on the outside, with the shield's M emblem now seared into its head. It looked like a Happy Meal. Its skin glistened. Jack assumed it had been in the downstairs loo, dousing its burning flesh with handfuls of toilet water. Consequently, the fire inside its head had diminished.

But not extinguished.

The jack-o'-lantern yapped in anger, like a feisty terrier, and hurtled across the lounge, bowling Jack over. The demon pinned Jack to the ground. It looked ready to bite Jack with its triangular, carved teeth. Jack pushed upwards with both hands to keep the pumpkin-head at bay. Ridiculously, his hands still clutched the skull, meaning he was now looking up at two mouths bearing down on him, both trying to bite him.

Worse, the jack-o'-lantern seemed to be getting a kick from the attack and its fire started to burn brighter once again. It opened its mouth. The air shimmered with heat.

'Sheriff!' shouted Jack.

But the Sheriff was busy. It fought the rest of the skeleton, his sword clanging against the skeleton's bone-sword. The skeleton was taller and wider now, having spread out its floating bones, which meant it towered over the Sheriff.

The Sheriff's need for help appeared greater than his own, but what could Jack do?

Wait, the book!

Whispers of cloud poured from the open copy of *The Sheriff*, lying forgotten on the carpet. The skeleton had stepped through it. This was the Sheriff's way home. A portal to the clouds.

Jack was reminded of a joke –

The jack-o'-lantern pressed down on him, which in turn pushed the skull in Jack's hands down towards him. The jack-o'-lantern's fiery breath intensified. One bite from the pumpkin's mouth would do more than take a chunk out of him. It would melt his skin –

Now or never.

Jack removed his right hand from the jack-o'-lantern, leaving all hope of keeping the demon at bay with his left hand, which now gripped the fiery demon by the throat. It didn't go well. The demon descended instantly, its mouth suddenly inches from his face.

But his right hand, still desperately gripping the skull, was now free to move.

He stretched out.

'Why didn't – '

Sought the open copy of *The Sheriff*.

' – the skeleton – '

Raised the skull in his hand.

' – go to the ball?'

And brought it down onto the book's open pages.

The skull vanished, as though tossed down a well.

With the head gone, the rest of the skeleton's body instantly fell to pieces. Whatever hex had been holding it together had been cut off. The signal was lost. The Sheriff looked confused by the disintegration of its enemy, then glimpsed the open book, the placement of Jack's hand, and understood. Luckily, the Sheriff thought and moved fast because –

The jack-o'-lantern opened its mouth, its fire burning white-hot. Jack felt his skin burn.

Squelch.

The top half of the jack-o'-lantern's head vanished. Its fire died. The mouth was all that remained of the pumpkin-head. It drooped into a forlorn look of surprise. The Sheriff booted the jack-o'-lantern backwards and its body hit the carpet, lifeless.

Jack and the Sheriff panted heavily. They warily watched the demons' bodies, Jack still on his back and the Sheriff standing with a pumpkin-soaked sword. They broke the silence at the same time with the same words.

'Thank you.'

Turn to page 252.

Chapter 80

Everything was dark.

Jack could feel his consciousness slowly awake, clawing its way to the surface, as though wading upwards through a thick puddle of tar, or demonic gloop, or Jäger –

A slap helped speed things up.

'Wake up, human,' said Balam.

Jack gasped in shock, sucking in deep breaths of the night air. His head felt worse than it ever had. The result of being batted by a bear, or an early Jägermeister hangover? It was hard to say. Probably the former, although he had been to enough Jägerbomb nights to suspect otherwise.

'Eustace!' Jack called, remembering his companion.

'Right here,' said the saint.

Eustace was tied up with coarse rope, dumped on the grass. Balam stood over him. The hawk perched nearby on a slipshod bird table, watching intently. Jack was tied up too, only he was upright, his feet dangling pathetically above the ground. Looking down, he realised that it wasn't rope which bound him. It was the bear's arms. The creature held him tightly from behind, as though it wore a baby carrier and Jack was its offspring.

'We're still alive?' said Jack.

'Not for long,' answered Balam.

'All of this for a little sugar,' said Eustace, tutting.

'Sugar?' cackled Balam. 'Don't confuse me with those three imps. The imps are gone. You saw to that. They left behind three empty vessels for me to possess, one for each of my heads. Seemed like too good an opportunity to miss, especially on Halloween.'

'What *do* you want?' asked Eustace.

'I'm going to get my kicks torturing the patron saint of torture victims. That's one of yours, isn't it, Eustace?'

Eustace nodded, resigned.

Balan was delighted. 'Let's see if you're as robust as your patronage implies. The human can watch.

I'm curious to see which of you will scream first.'

'Sadist monster,' said Eustace.

'Of course,' said Balam, with a shrug. 'You see the horns, right?'

Eustace sat up straight. 'Do your worst, demon.'

'I won't need my worst, saint. This human has no faith.' Jack reddened. 'Your divine powers are dwindling.'

'I do believe in him,' said Jack, although a lifetime of atheism was hard to overturn, despite the events unfolding before his eyes.

Balam grinned, with all six of his mouths. 'I guess we'll find out.' The demon towered over Eustace, eyes aglow. 'Now then, o' mighty patron saint of torture victims. I wonder how long you can hold your breath.'

His snake-tail wrapped around Eustace's neck. The snake was impossibly long, coiling round and round, before squeezing tightly. Eustace choked. The head of the snake settled in front of Eustace's bloodshot eyes, its own eyes glowing as fiery as those in Balam's head.

'No, don't, leave him,' pleaded Jack.

Balam squeezed until Eustace's eyes were bulging from their sockets.

'Stop!'

The saint's face grew purple, his mouth open and gasping for air, out of which protruded his hard and rigid tongue.

'Stop, please!'

Balam laughed. The snake relinquished, albeit just enough to let Eustace heave in a big mouthful of cool night air. Its scaly body never left the saint's neck, poised for another bout, like a reptilian snood.

'How was that, Eustace?' asked Balam, brightly.

Eustace sucked in more air before fixing the demon with a glare. 'That was it?'

Balam's grin fell. 'No, saint. That was round one. Let's go for longer.'

The snake gave a frisson of joy and started tightening.

Jack had to do something –

To scream for help, turn to page 282.

To buy some time, turn to page 181.

Chapter 81

Wait, the mummy?

Jack recalled the shield landing somewhere near the mummy. *Now, where is it?*

He searched around himself, feeling blindly, because his eyes never left the advancing skeleton. Thankfully, his fingers felt metal. He brought the shield up in front of him – clang – parrying the first blow, yet the second attack once again disarmed him. The shield vanished from his hands.

Still, its brief intervention had allowed the Sheriff a few extra seconds to come to Jack's aid. The lion-man launched the decapitated jack-o'-lantern's head at the skeleton with fearsome force. The weighty squash knocked the demon off its feet.

'To me!' cried the Sheriff.

The lounge was aflame. Jack and the Sheriff positioned themselves in the middle, away from the fiery walls. It was also where the sword and shield had landed after being whipped from Jack's hands. The Sheriff picked them up and armed himself. Jack sheltered behind him.

The skeleton stood, grinning, always grinning, but somehow more now. It clicked its fingers and the headless jack-o'-lantern and equally headless mummy rose from the carpet. Each retrieved their own heads and wedged them back onto their necks.

'Oh, that's not fair,' whined Jack, breathless from the thinning air.

'Little is,' said the Sheriff.

'I don't want to die at the hands of trick-or-treaters.'

'The fire might get us first.'

'That's not helping.'

A chunk of burning ceiling crashed into the room, only a few feet away from the mummy.

'The fire might get them too,' noted the Sheriff.

The skeleton advanced slowly, step by step, flanked by its associates. 'I told you,' it cackled. 'Curiosity killed the cat.'

The Sheriff growled. 'And I told you, I'm not a cat.'

Jack felt a cold draught on his leg. Coolness was so alien in that smouldering room, that it stole his attention away from the three demons.

Jack stared. There was smoke on the floor, only this smoke was white in colour and cool against his ankle. On closer inspection, Jack realised it wasn't smoke at all, but rather wisps of cloud, pouring from the open pages of a book. He could guess which book too.

He bent down and pushed his hand through the cloud. It passed through the pages of the book too, as though he was reaching into a hole. A deep hole.

'Not a cat,' repeated the skeleton, advancing. 'What are you then?'

'He's a Sheriff,' Jack answered.

Jack grabbed the Sheriff by the back of his armour and yanked him into the expanding pool of swirling cloud. The Sheriff dropped from sight, as though he had stepped into a pit. Jack was left alone with the three demons and his collapsing house.

Not for long.

'Happy Halloween,' he declared, jumping after the Sheriff. His last glimpse of his lounge saw another chunk of burning ceiling falling towards the demons.

And then –

Turn to page 259.

Chapter 82

'Balam?' repeated Jack.

'A Duke of Hell,' explained Eustace, eyes lingering on the burning fence at the back of the garden. Jack could read his thoughts. Their escape route had gone up in flames. 'He commands over forty legions of demons. Powerful but smart too. It is said that Balam gives perfect answers to all things past, present and future. A demon renowned for his humour and wit.'

'Not to mention its three heads,' guessed Jack, peering at the demon over the wheelbarrow. 'Anything else I should know?'

'Other than that, he has all the usual demon traits.'

'Meaning?'

'He is arrogant, proud, competitive, unable to resist a wager.'

The three heads remained as they were, sat atop

the shape-shifting blob of black gloop. The bull and ram's heads shifted upwards on the man's head until he was wearing them like a tricorn hat, their horns pointing outwards. The man's red eyes grew brighter and brighter, whilst the life in the eyes of the bull and ram died, as though they were now nothing more than stuffed and mounted trophies.

Finally, the black gloop settled on a form.

The three-headed demon's body was human for the most part. His upper half was naked, muscular and taut, though criss-crossed with a thousand cuts. His legs may have been naked too, though it was impossible to tell on account of the shaggy fur that covered him below the waist.

But that wasn't all.

'Caw!'

The demon had a hawk on his arm, its talons gripping tightly, beak sharp, eyes glinting, eager to fly.

'Hiss!'

The demon had a snake for a tail, which rose high and peered over his shoulder, keen to see its closest source of human flesh.

'Roar!'

And whilst the hawk and snake were monstrous, they were nothing compared to the creature upon which it sat. Between its legs, the demon rode a ferocious, grizzly bear, with dark matted fur, enormous clawed paws, and a drooling maw of teeth.

Eustace spoke first. 'Finish the Jäger! I need as much faith fuel as possible.'

'I have!' said Jack.

'Are you sure?'

'Yes!' He waved the empty green bottle in Eustace's face. 'See!'

Oh god, the Jäger. The black, horrid liquid was sloshing around in his stomach. He pictured it now, then pictured the shimmering black gloop from which Balam had formed. The gloop had smelled rancid. He could still smell it –

'Oh, no.'

Jack bent double and retched.

For a not-so-tactical chunder, turn to page 166.

To keep the Jäger down, turn to page 196.

Chapter 83

'Help! Please, somebody help!' screamed Jack.

'Be quiet, human,' cursed Balam.

'Call the police! Call the army! Call everyone!'

'No, no, no,' said the demon, shaking his three heads. 'How am I supposed to administer torture with that horrible racket going on?'

Jack continued screaming all the same. 'Help! Somebody exorcise this demon! I need a priest! I need the pope!'

'Enough.'

The demon clicked his fingers. The hawk sprang into action, vacating its perch and soaring straight at Jack. His arms were still pinned to his side by the bear, so he couldn't protect his face with his hands.

In one swift movement, the hawk swooped past Jack's exposed throat and tore out his vocal cords.

Oh!

When the hawk returned to its perch, the chords

dangled from its talons like linguini.

That manoeuvre had put an end to Jack's shouting.

It had also put an end to Jack.

Blood gushed, unchecked, from his torn throat. His life poured away. At the very least, he hoped that his cries for help had been heard by someone who would come and save Eustace.

Jack, however, was beyond saving. He had reached

THE END.

Chapter 84

'Help! Help!' screamed Jack. 'I'm being held hostage by a demon and his pets!'

That was one hell of a sentence.

'Silence, human,' snapped Balam. 'I'm trying to concentrate. Torture requires the utmost care.'

Jack ignored the demon. 'He has a bear and a hawk and a snake! Send animal control! Send a zoo keeper! Send a taxidermist!'

'I won't tell you again,' warned Balam.

'Somebody, anybody, help!'

'That's it. I've changed my mind. I don't need a witness to make this fun.'

Balam nodded at the bear. The creature growled excitedly. It gripped Jack's head tightly, twisted and yanked it upwards. It popped off as easily as the head of a Lego figure. The bear held it aloft in both hands, like the FA cup.

'That's better,' said Balam.

The bear grew bored of Jack's head just as quickly and tossed it over its shoulder.

As Jack's head rolled to a standstill in the grass, he recalled being told that the human head remains conscious for ten seconds after decapitation, after which brain ischemia kicks in.

Ten, nine.

Long enough to dwell on his mistakes.

Eight, seven.

Screaming had been a bad idea. He should have kept the demon talking.

Six, five.

If only he hadn't been sick.

Four, three.

Maybe he should have reached for Joan's favourite book instead.

Two, one.

He never should have answered the door.

...

THE END

Chapter 85

Joan walked up the garden, eyes full of wonder and confusion, flitting between her trapped husband, the bear, the tortured saint with the glowing halo, and the three-headed, snake-tailed, fiery-eyed demon. She approached warily, with her police baton and pepper spray in hand.

'What is happening here?'

Jack mumbled a reply into the bear's paw.

'Never mind,' said Joan. 'You! Step back!'

Balam appraised the new arrival. 'Another human.' The hawk returned to Balam's wrist and surveyed her itself. 'You can watch too. The torture was just getting interesting, wasn't it, Eustace?'

'You're Balam,' said Joan. Her biblical studies meant that she was much better-versed in demonology than Jack. 'And you must be Saint Eustace?'

'That's right,' said the saint, catching his breath,

recomposing himself.

Jack observed Eustace carefully. His halo was glowing again, brighter and whiter. The wounds on his neck and scalp were healing too. It was Joan. Someone of faith had arrived and it was working wonders for Eustace's divine powers. Her lifetime of Church-going, Bible-reading, Sunday school, and unwavering belief surged into Eustace and gave him the strength he needed.

'Put your toys down,' said Balam, as Joan stepped closer, with her baton and pepper spray. 'Or I will take them and use them on you.'

'Is that right?' said Joan.

Balam lunged at Joan but she stood her ground. She placed her can of pepper spray horizontally over her upheld baton, forming a cross. Instantly, the cross lit up with the same bright, white glow as Eustace's halo. The demon recoiled with a hiss.

Jack expected the rejuvenated Eustace to rip free of his bonds. Instead, the saint tilted his head to the sky and closed his eyes.

The bear had thankfully uncovered Jack's mouth, its attention now on Joan, along with the rest of

Balam's selves. It allowed Jack to issue an urgent whisper to the saint.

'Eustace, wake up. My wife needs help.'

'I told you,' said Eustace, his eyes still closed. 'I'm not just the patron saint of hunting.'

'Are you the patron saint of meditation now too?'

'No, but I am the patron saint of firefighters.'

Jack looked to the fence at the top of his garden, still burning from its encounter with the jack-o-lantern's fireball much earlier that evening.

'Don't worry about the fire,' said Jack. 'Worry about Joan.'

'Listen.'

The sound of an engine could be heard overhead. 'What is that? Did you summon a plane?'

'Not just a plane. An air tanker.'

'A what?'

The red plane came into view, flying towards their garden. It was decorated much like a fire engine, with a red coat of paint and blue flashing lights. Jack understood now. An air tanker was one of those fire-fighting planes that flew over forest fires to drop gallons of water onto the blaze.

And here it comes now.

The belly of the plane opened up to unleash a deluge of water. It poured down towards the spot where they were gathered. The water would fall short of the burning fence at the top of the garden.

'Are you doing this?' he asked Eustace, but the saint simply stared up at the approaching water, speaking quickly under his breath.

'Water?' laughed Balam, arms outstretched to welcome the shower. 'It will take more than that to extinguish the fire in my eyes.'

'Not water,' said Jack, 289ueled289ng what Eustace was muttering. 'Holy water.'

Balam's grin dropped.

The water struck.

Jack, Joan, Eustace and Balam were knocked flat against the ground. The impact hurt – that volume of water was heavy – but it was so much worse for Balam, who instantly started sizzling.

'Argh!'

The hawk vanished first. The water plastered it against the ground, where it became a molten puddle of feathers. The bear roared, its flesh melting from its body, before collapsing in on itself. Balam had become a staggering skeleton, with three skulls gaping atop its shoulders, and a thrashing spine where its snake-tail used to be. The bones were softening too, wilting, crumpling.

'You – '

The demon pointed at Jack and Eustace, only it could say no more because the bottom half of its jaw dropped away.

Eustace's halo glowed brighter than ever, 290ueled by the arrival of Joan and her faith. He finally ripped his hands free of the binding rope, as though it were tissue paper, and rose to his feet. He held out both hands and each half of his broken bow flew to him, before miraculously reforming.

'Arrow,' said Eustace.

Jack leapt to his own feet and obliged the saint, selecting one from Eustace's quiver.

Balam took a shaky but threatening step towards Eustace, hand outstretched. Eustace drew the arrow –

But it wasn't needed.

Balam's head disappeared.

A swift swing from Joan's baton had knocked it from the demon's shoulders.

'Be gone, demon,' commanded Joan. Balam's body made a half-hearted attempt to turn and face its attacker – face, perhaps, no longer being the right word to use – but it collapsed into a stew of gloopy bones. 'And stay gone.'

Jack ran forward and embraced his wife, both drenched to the bone from the air tanker's payload of water. The tanker itself now circled back and doused the flames rising from the garden fence, which extinguished in a plume of dirty smoke.

'You came for me,' said Jack, holding his wife tightly. 'I knew you would. I believe in you, Joan.'

'I leave you alone for one night,' said Joan, catching her breath. 'And I come home to find a demon and a saint in our garden.'

'Don't forget the bear.'

'How could I?'

Eustace approached the couple. 'Thank you, Joan. A timely intervention. Divine, even.'

'Someone has to keep an eye on this one,' she said, patting her husband.

'You'd make a good saint yourself,' said Eustace. 'But we already have a Joan.'

'My wife is named after her,' said Jack.

'A fitting choice.'

'Thank you,' said Joan. 'But I don't need a sainthood to keep me busy.' She put an arm around Jack. 'I have a marriage.'

THE END

Chapter 86

Balam asked his first riddle. 'He who makes it, has no need of it. He who buys it, has no use for it. He who uses it, can neither see nor feel it. What is it?'

'A coffin,' answered Jack without hesitation.

Balam's flaming eyes widened in surprise.

Jack smirked. *Didn't expect that, did you?*

Since buying an Amazon Echo a year ago, Jack had made use of the smart speaker's riddle function several times a day. He now knew hundreds of riddles off by heart. Balam might have met his match.

'Yes, correct, a coffin,' said Balam, grudgingly. His mood darkened. 'You'll need one yourself before this night is through.'

Jack's smirk died on his lips. He could kick himself for answering so quickly. The whole point of this game was to buy time. He couldn't afford to make that mistake again.

'Okay, my turn,' he said. 'Imagine you are in a dark room. How do you get out?'

'Stop imagining,' said Balam, immediately. Jack was disappointed. He had thought that riddle would at least give the demon pause for thought. Balam moved on, as eager for this to be over, as Jack was to drag it out. 'What can travel around the world without ever leaving the corner?'

Jack stopped himself this time. He knew the answer, of course, but he resisted blurting it out, despite wanting to see the look of disappointment on Balam's face.

'Hmm,' he feigned. 'Without ever leaving the corner?'

Balam's sharp-toothed grin widened, as Jack continued to make confused expressions.

'You don't know,' said Balam.

'Give me a second.'

A little more time passed. Eventually, the demon lost patience. 'Last chance. Three, two, one – '

'A stamp!' cried Jack, triumphantly.

Balam fumed. 'Yes,' he conceded.

'My turn to ask,' said Jack. 'Let me think.' Another opportunity for Jack to stretch out the game. He pretended to be thinking of a riddle, when he actually had a dozen on the tip of his tongue.

'Get on with it.'

'No, I want to ask a good one.'

Balam stamped his foot in annoyance. 'If you can't think of one, then I win this round.'

'Okay, okay. Which word in the dictionary is spelt inconsistently?'

'Inconsistently,' answered Balam, correctly, before ploughing on. 'Feed me and I grow. Give me a drink and I die. What am I?'

Bugger.

Jack actually didn't know. Well, he did, it was familiar, but his mind was blank. *Oh, come on Jack, think.* But it was hard to think when a bear was squeezing him tightly and a Duke of Hell was leering at him.

'I don't have all day, human,' goaded Balam, eyes burning triumphantly. Jack stared into those flaming eyes –

And there was the answer.

'Fire!' he cried.

Balam folded his arms. 'Yes, fire. Where you'll be spending eternity.'

'We'll see about that.'

The game continued. Balam lived up to his reputation as a demon of wit. He rattled off answers to Jack's questions without a moment's thought. Often, Balam didn't even need to hear the entire question.

'What does a butcher – '

'Meat.'

'What has hands but – '

'Clock.'

'What has an eye but – '

'Needle.'

'What kind of room – '

'Mushroom.'

It put more pressure on Jack to stall for time, pretending he didn't know the answers, even though he did. However, there were plenty of times when he didn't have to pretend. Some of the demon's riddles were ones which Jack had never heard before – fiendishly difficult ones too.

'If you have me, you want to share me. If you share me, I no longer exist.'

'I am as light as a feather but cannot be held.'

'I appear once in a minute, twice in a moment, but never in a thousand years.'

All of the above had stumped Jack for a good long while, before he correctly answered 'secret' and 'breath' and 'the letter M.' He had genuinely needed every last second for that final riddle, answering at the same moment that Balam counted down to one.

Still, the game remained a draw.

But then –

'Three men are on a boat,' began Balam, grinning wider than usual. Jack gulped. He wondered if the demon had been saving this one. 'They have a packet of cigarettes but no lighter. How do they smoke?'

Crap.

He had no idea.

Turn to page 314.

Chapter 87

'A double-barrel Super Soaker XXP 175,' said Jack.

It was a yellow-purple-red weapon with pump action and a water pressure gauge. He had wielded this model with aplomb as a child. Jack picked it up, feeling the familiar weight. It had probably been in the shed for years, but he spied water sloshing around in the twin barrels.

Jack wasn't sure if hawks liked water.

But he had a feeling that demonic hell-birds didn't like holy water.

'God, please bless this water and make it holy,' he improvised. 'Please?'

The door disappeared behind him. The hawk's talons had torn it free. The bird now shook the ruined wood from its talons. Jack allowed it no time to compose itself. He pumped the Super Soaker, whilst charging at the bird, screaming and squirting.

'Take that!'

The pistol soaked the bird superbly. It darted upwards to escape the spray, screeching in fury –

– but not in pain.

'Ah.' Still just regular water then. 'But I said please!' he shouted to the stars.

The bird stared down at Jack, seething, shaking the tepid water from its wings.

'Um. Sorry?'

The hawk tilted its head, as if to say: *Like water, do you? Well, now it's your turn to get wet.* It was a *very* expressive tilt of its head. The bird dived at Jack one last time –

Jack raised the Super Soaker to protect his face from the talons, but the hawk targeted the back of his jumper instead. It hauled Jack into the air with a strength far surpassing that of a regular hawk. Jack dropped the Super Soaker in surprise and it quickly became a small dot beneath him as the hawk carried him into the sky.

'Wait, stop!' he cried, uselessly. 'Where are you taking me?'

There was no reply, but Jack soon saw for himself. The pond.

It was yet another leftover from the previous owners, which Jack and Joan had spent no time on maintaining.

'Eustace! Help! The pond!'

Far below, the saint avoided another charge from the bear, then looked up. 'You have a pond? Where?'

'Here!' screamed Jack, as the hawk released him. He screamed all the way down and landed with a splash in the green, swampy water. It was deep and full of spongey algae and weeds, which undoubtedly saved him from a broken neck. He surfaced and splashed around, spluttering, thankful to still draw breath.

But his relief didn't last long. The hawk landed on his back, hard, and pushed him under the water.

And held him there.

Turn to page 338.

Chapter 88

Jack knew it had to be a good riddle, but once again his mind had gone blank. In fact, forget about coming up with a good one. Right now, he couldn't think of a single riddle. The pressure was like a vice on his chest. Or maybe that was the bear.

'Better make it count, human,' teased Balam. 'Your soul is resting on the line. An eternity of torture awaits if I answer correctly. God won't be able to save you once the Devil owns your soul.'

The taunt stirred a memory.

A riddle presented itself to him, conjured up by the demon's words. As to whether it would be difficult to answer, he had no way of knowing. But it was the only riddle he had. Jack had no choice to ask it, otherwise he would lose by default.

'What is greater than God?' he asked. 'More evil than the Devil? The poor have it, the rich need it, and if you eat it, you'll die?'

Silence.

Balam eyeballed him in thought, giving nothing away.

Eventually, he said, 'Greater than God? Many things are greater than God. What is so great about God? He just sits in the Heavens, staying out of it. More evil than the Devil? That's assuming that the Devil is evil. You haven't heard his side of it.'

The faintest glimmer of hope stirred within Jack. He sincerely hoped Balam wasn't toying with him.

'The poor have it?' continued Balam, now pacing, rubbing his three heads in thought. 'Disease? Misery? Desperation? And the rich need it? What do they need? A good slap every now and then?'

Jack's glimmer of hope started to glow brighter.

'And if you eat it, you'll die?' the demon roared in Jack's face. 'What does that mean? Poison? Glass? Fire?'

Again with the fire!

'Nettles? Thumbtacks? Tarantulas?'

Jack's only response was a smile and the words, 'Three, two, one – '

'Don't you dare count at me!' shrieked Balam, fire

spurting from his eyes, his nostrils, his mouth.

'Time is up,' said Jack steadily. 'I win.'

Balam stared.

Jack added, louder this time, realisation sinking in, 'I win! You have to let me go!'

The demon's look of shock morphed into one of the utmost evil.

'Do I?'

'Yes, you said.'

'Horns, remember?' Balam gestured. 'Demons aren't big on honesty.'

'No, that's not fair. I won.'

The bear tightened its paws on either side of Jack's head, ready to pull.

'No,' he protested.

'I do love Halloween,' said Balam, gleefully watching Jack panic.

In the distance, the church bells rang.

Midnight.

'It isn't Halloween any more,' said Jack, just before the paws could pull upwards.

The bear froze. Its paws withdrew. Balam stared at Jack.

'What did you say?'

Something dropped from the sky and slammed into the ground beside Balam. The mighty Duke of Hell shrieked in surprise and jumped aside. It was a metal cylinder, spiralling down, like a helter-skelter from the Heavens.

'No, no,' cursed the demon, as another cylinder followed, then another, and another. The bear roared and backed away on all fours. The hawk flapped in distress. The snake-tail coiled up close to Balam's back to avoid being crushed.

Not cylinders, realised Jack on closer inspection. Metal staircases, with the steps spiralling tightly, framed by an ornate metal railing.

'Stairways,' said Balam, all six pairs of eyes darting left and right in panic. More thudded into the ground around him, descending from the stars.

'Stairways from Heaven,' corrected Eustace, having regained consciousness. The saint looked different. He was bathed in light. Jack realised the saint's halo was glowing brighter and whiter than ever.

'How is this possible?' shouted Balam.

'It's not Halloween anymore,' said Jack. 'It's the first day of November.'

'What?'

'All Saint's Day.'

Turn to page 342.

Chapter 89

Jack slowly looked up.

The face of the decrepit mummy leered down at him.

It had lowered itself from the canopy of overhead branches, using one of its own bandages as a rope, like a spider on a web. The mummy reached for Jack's face.

'Eustace!'

The rope attached to Jack's midriff pulled taut and Jack was reeled backwards. Another of Eustace's makeshift mechanisms. An arrow flew from the woods, slicing through the bandage on which the mummy had descended with impeccable accuracy.

The mummy fell onto the spot where Jack had been sat. Huge, metal teeth snapped up from the ground and clamped shut on the mummy.

SNAP.

The mummy burst apart in the metal jaws,

severed in two. Each half crumbled to dust.

'Damn, Eustace,' panted Jack. 'I was sitting on that thing?'

The saint's glowing halo blinkered into life again, revealing his location. He stepped forward from the tree line.

'You're welcome by the way.'

Jack only had eyes for the enormous metal trap. 'I don't even know where you got that thing. Was it in your pocket?'

Eustace shrugged. 'I'm not just the patron saint of hunting. I'm the patron saint of trappers too.'

'So you can just magic these things out of thin air?'

The saint made a so-so motion with his hand. 'Only when people believe in me. You started to have faith after I brought down the first two demons.'

'I did?'

'You did.'

'But how did you know the trap wasn't going to snap shut on me?'

'I guessed your weight.'

'Guessed?'

'I guessed the weight of the demons too. They're surprisingly dense for such little buggers. Only their weight would have triggered my traps.'

'Guessed?'

'Well, calculated. I'm good with numbers.'

Jack stared.

'I'm also the patron saint for mathematicians, remember?'

Eustace bent down to untie Jack's ropes, whilst Jack's heartbeat returned to normal. His fingers barely touched the knot before –

'Gak!'

The elevated net burst open. The skeleton fell to earth in a shower of dirt and leaves. It hit the ground at a sprint, making a beeline for Jack and Eustace.

'Eustace!'

The saint stood, drew his bow, and loosed an arrow in haste. But the saint was accustomed to taking his time, a hunter, not a warrior, and the arrow missed the skeleton by an inch. There was no time for Eustace to draw a second arrow.

The skeleton ran over its fallen associate in the

metal trap, empty sockets fixated on its prey, sharp fingers ready at its side –

And the ground fell away beneath its feet.

'Gak!'

The demon dropped from view. The mummy and metal trap dropped with it.

Jack stared, dumbfounded yet again. 'Another trap? I was sat on top of a pit, as well?'

'No,' said Eustace, slowly. 'You were sat on branches and leaves. The pit was underneath.'

'But how did you – ?'

'Maths.'

'But – '

'Maths.'

Jack gave up. 'What if it climbs out?'

'It won't. Here.'

Eustace untied Jack and helped him to his feet. He led him over to the edge of the pit. Looking down, Jack saw the skeleton skewered on sharpened sticks. No, not just sticks. Crosses.

Their sharp tips shone with the same glow as Eustace's halo. Each had punched a hole in the skeleton, who lay motionless.

'Christ,' said Jack.

'Exactly.'

'Thank you, Eustace. I should count my blessings.'

'I can help you with that.'

'What?'

'Counting.' Eustace slapped Jack on the back. 'Did I mention I'm the patron saint of mathematicians?'

THE END

Chapter 90

Jack dived to the ground, but not quickly enough. The hell-bird's talons scraped his skull.

'Ow, what the hell?'

Jack leapt to his feet and sprinted away, whilst the bird looped overhead for another attack. Jack searched the garden wildly as he ran. Where to go? Greenhouse? Shed? Hide behind the water butt?

'Caw!'

'Shit!' Jack dived a second time, landing heavily on his front. The impact knocked the air from his lungs. The time, the hawk missed him completely, thankfully, luckily, but the venomous screech issued from its beak told Jack that it was more vexed than ever.

The shed is closest. Definitely the shed.

He rose again, slower, but fear soon got his legs moving. His eyes fixed on the shed. It had a door. He could slam that in the hawk's face.

Run, run, run, run –

The rushing of wings sliced through the air behind him.

Ten feet, five feet, hand on the door handle –

'Caw!'

Jack made it, slamming the wooden door behind him. Ten talons immediately punched through the thin wood like throwing knives.

'Jesus,' cursed Jack. Those talons had almost sunk into his face. He stumbled backwards in shock, although there wasn't really any room to stumble backwards. The elderly couple who previously owned his house had used the greenhouse to store most of their tools, scrap, and garden chemicals. The shed was tiny by comparison, no bigger than a Portaloo. Instead of tools, it was piled with garden toys, presumably for visiting grandchildren.

The door shuddered behind Jack. The hawk was trying to pull its talons free. Judging by the door's rusted hinges, the door might be yanked free with them.

Outside, Jack could hear Eustace's cries of 'Hyah!' and 'Olé!' The saint was busy. No help would come from there.

Jack needed a weapon. His eyes rapidly scanned the items in the shed: Jenga blocks, boules, plastic golf clubs, foam baseball bats, tossing rings – all dirty, grimy, mouldy. The baseball bat was tempting, the ball-on-a-string pole too, but then Jack spotted something better.

Turn to page 298.

Chapter 91

Jack felt his heart sink. It was unlike any riddle he had heard before. *Think, think, think,* he told himself. It didn't help that Balam had been intimidating him throughout the game, purposefully psyching him out, with threatening responses to Jack's riddles, for instance –

'Take off my skin – I won't cry but you will.'

'An onion,' said Balam, correctly, before adding, 'Maybe I will remove your skin after I beat you. Then we'll see who cries.'

With threats like that, no wonder Jack couldn't think straight.

'Three, two, one,' taunted Balam.

'Wait!'

'Time's up.'

'No!' shouted Jack, frustrated. 'What is the answer? How do they smoke?'

'The three men throw a cigarette overboard.'

'What?'

'And the entire boat becomes a cigarette lighter.'

Jack stared. 'What the – Oh, come on, that's a trick question.'

Balam laughed. 'This is game of riddles. They are all trick questions.'

The game continued. Jack was now very conscious that he was a point in arrears. Fresh inspiration struck when Balam asked, 'I'm tall when I'm young and short when I'm old. What am I?'

Jack knew the answer was 'candle' and eventually answered as such, but he also realised that it was the demon's second question with a flame-related answer. Are all demons obsessed with flames? If so, maybe they have a blind spot for water riddles? Surely, there isn't much water in Hell?

Jack gave it a shot. 'What gets wetter and wetter the more it dries?'

For the first time, Balam hesitated. Jack held his breath as the demon slowly frowned, the confusion spreading across his face, like ripples in a pond. He watched the demon's mouth form and then re-form into a series of shapes, on the verge of trying different answers and then deciding better of it.

Eventually, Balam said, 'Can you repeat the question?'

Jack would have punched the air in joy had his arms not been pinned to his side. 'Three, two, one.'

'Stop counting, human!'

'Time's up! The answer is a towel!'

'A what?' Balam formed a fist and slammed it into the ground. The entire garden shook. Jack barely noticed. He had cost the demon a point. They were drawing again.

The game moved on. Both Jack and Balam held their own with a series of challenging riddles and correct answers. Jack continued to stall for time with his false musings to each of the demon's questions. Still, the best way to stretch out the game was if Jack stayed *in* the game.

Riddle after riddle after riddle.

'What type of tree can you hold in your hand?'

'What has a head and a tail but no body?'

'What has four legs, two legs and three legs?'

Jack very nearly slipped up again, when Balam had asked, 'Forwards, I am heavy. Backwards, I am not. What am I?'

Jack even agonised into countdown territory, but at the last second it clicked. 'Ton!' he declared.

Balam nodded with a growl. 'Almost had you.'

'That because we don't spell it T-O-N over here,' protested Jack. 'That's the American spelling. Are all demons American?'

'What do you think?'

'I think your leaders have a lot in common.'

Finally, they reached riddle number thirty, still at a draw. It was Balam's turn to ask. 'How many species of animal did Moses take on the Ark?'

Oh, no.

A biblical riddle. This would have been Joan's turn to shine, had she been here. She was the devout Christian, not him. Was it forty? Forty was definitely something to do with Noah's Ark. Or did he mishear the question? Was it how many of *each* species did Noah take on the Ark? Was the answer two? But no, he replayed the question in his head. Balam had definitely asked how many species.

A lone synapse in Jack's brain gave him a poke.

Moses.

What was that?

Moses.

Hang on a second.

Moses.

Isn't Moses the parting-of-the-sea guy?

His eyes lit up.

'Trick question! Trick question!' he shouted. 'None! Moses didn't take any species of animal onto the Ark because it was *Noah's* Ark!'

Balam's face fell from rising smugness to crushing disappointment. He swore in a language that Jack had never heard, uttering some foul profanity from the inner circles of Hell. The demon punched the ground again, this time hard enough to shatter the greenhouse on the other side of the garden.

'Yes,' the demon said quietly. 'You are correct.'

And that was how they found themselves at riddle number thirty-one.

The last riddle.

The decider.

And it was Jack's turn to ask.

Turn to page 301.

Chapter 92

'There you are!' said Balam. The demon had dismounted from his bear, marched into the greenhouse, and found Jack crouched over the tap. 'Out we go.'

Balam dragged Jack outside, across the garden, and threw him onto the grass beside Eustace. The saint was in a bad way. His torso bled, courtesy of a bite-mark from the bear.

'Eustace, you're hurt,' said Jack.

'If I had my bow,' began Eustace, wincing.

'What happened to your bow?'

'The bear snapped it.'

'Cut the chatter,' demanded Balam, pacing in front of them. 'Now that we're all together again, the fun can begin. Human, you can watch me torture your new friend.'

Jack ignored the demon, whispering to Eustace, 'You're a saint, right?'

'Did the halo give me away?'

'Can you bless tap water? Make it holy?'

'Yes. You got any water?'

'It's coming.'

Balam snarled and knocked both of their heads together. Jack and Eustace swore.

'Stop whispering,' demanded Balam. 'You are in the presence of a Duke of Hell. You will give me your respect.'

It was time.

'How about we give you a bath instead?' said Jack.

The sprinklers awoke.

Cold water showered them all. Balam barely registered any surprise. The demon merely laughed. 'This is your defence? Water?'

But Eustace's eyes were closed. He spoke quickly under his breath.

Balam glared. 'I told you to stop whispering!' The demon brought back his arm, ready to deliver a brutal backhand –

And howled in agony.

The water from the sprinklers suddenly had a different effect on the demon. Once an annoyance, the droplets were now causing Balam to shriek with pain. He recoiled from the spray. Jack was reminded of many mornings when he had stepped into the shower without testing the temperature first. Only, Balam couldn't dance away on this occasion because the sprinklers were everywhere.

Its skin became pockmarked like Swiss cheese, each droplet burning a hole, until there were too many holes and not enough skin. After that, big chunks of the demon's flesh fell away.

The water had the same effect on the bear too, which rolled around in agony.

'It's not enough water,' said Eustace.

'Not enough?' said Jack. 'Look, we're hurting him.'

'Hurting, not killing. I think we're just making him angry.'

'You're right about that,' roared Balam, jets of flame shooting from his eyes.

The bear found its four feet again and charged in a rage. Eustace shoved Jack, so he landed beside the relative safety of a sprinkler head. The bear went after Eustace, snatching up the saint in its jaws and shaking him like a ragdoll.

Balam laughed. Jack felt helpless. To make matters worse, the hawk had regained consciousness and returned to the fight. It dived towards Jack.

Turn to page 225.

Chapter 93

'Jack?' said a voice, gently shaking him.

'Huh?'

'Nice broomstick. I think witches are supposed to wear pointy hats.'

Jack jerked awake and saw a familiar face.

'Joan!'

'Hello love,' she said, still kitted out in her police uniform. She wore her domed custodian helmet, which made her look about a foot taller. 'Why do you have a broomstick? Did someone flour our driveway?'

'Flour?'

'That's the new one we've been dealing with,' sighed Joan. 'Reports of teenagers chucking torn bags of flour at people's houses. Harder to clean up than a broken egg. Halloween brings out all the monsters.'

'Tell me about it.'

'So *were* we floured?'

'Worse. Trick-or-treated.'

'How is that worse?'

'I ran out of treats.'

'I left you a whole bowl!'

'I know.'

'You ate it all, didn't you?'

'Not all.'

'So what did you give them?'

'I tried everything. Even your weight loss bars.'

'What?' She punched him on the arm. 'Those are expensive, Jack.'

'I'll buy you more. I'll buy you *lots* more.'

'I thought you hated them.'

'I can see they are a necessary evil.'

'Did the kids like them?'

'They ate them in one.'

'Good,' said Joan. 'Sounds like it all worked out.'

'One of them left me this,' said Jack, tapping his top hat. 'I like it.'

'I can see that,' said Joan, with a sigh. 'But you still haven't answered my question about the broomstick.'

'Ever the police officer,' said Jack. 'Can we just go inside?'

'I'll remove my hat if you remove yours.'

'Deal.'

Jack and Joan took off their hats and walked up their driveway, arms around each other.

'Long shift,' said Joan, yawning.

'Long night,' agreed Jack.

The pumpkin in the bay window spluttered out as they approached the house, falling into darkness. Maybe it knew that midnight had passed and Halloween was over.

'Hey, Joan,' said Jack. 'Why didn't the skeleton go to the ball?'

Joan groaned. 'Save it for next Halloween.'

THE END

Chapter 94

'Seriously?' said the demon. 'Apple-bobbing?'

'I mean, if you don't know – '

Balam's anger flared. The bear hugged Jack tighter.

'Of course, I know.'

'Go on.'

'It is a British courting ritual brought over by your Roman ancestors, popular for hundreds of years,' explained Balam, growling the explanation. 'Each apple in the barrel was assigned to a young man. The women would attempt to bite the apple assigned to the man they loved. If a woman bit the apple on her first attempt, then the young man was her destiny. If she bit the apple on her second attempt, they would court, but their love would fade. If it took three attempts or more, the couple were doomed.'

'I see.'

Balam showed his teeth. 'And if two people bumped heads over the barrel then they got dragged to Hell by a powerful and handsome demon.'

'Really?'

'We'll see,' threatened Balam. 'The night is still young.'

Yes, too young.

Jack needed to keep dragging this out. 'It sounds like more of a Valentine's Day thing,' he said, striving for conversation-starters. 'Nothing spooky about that.'

'Love is very hellish,' said Balam. 'Lust, greed, avarice – that's three sins, right there.'

'And that's why people bob for apples on Halloween?'

Balam sighed. 'Not quite.' The demon was frustrated by the game, but too proud to miss a chance to prove its knowledge. 'The Americans revived the game in the late nineteenth century. They were exploring their Celtic roots and discovered the festival of Samhain.'

'Of what?'

'Samhain. A celebration of the end of the harvest.

It takes place today on the thirty-first of October. The festival honours Pomona, the Roman goddess of fruit, represented by the apple. The game of apple-bobbing was thought to be a fitting tradition for such a day. Of course, nowadays, you mostly do it for fun.' Balam straightened up and cracked his knuckles. 'Speaking of which, it's time I had some fun of my own.'

The snake sprang into action, tightening one more around Eustace's throat. The saint thrashed and kicked his legs, mouth wide open, but unable to inhale.

Jack panicked. 'Wait! The future! The future!'

'What now?'

'Answers to all things, past, present and future.' Still, the snake held on. 'You've not answered any questions about the future.'

Balam stared at Jack, no doubt considering whether to end his interfering human life there and then. Instead, the demon cursed in a language Jack had never heard and let the snake fall slack again. He returned to Jack once more.

'The future is more difficult,' snapped Balam.

'Lots of different pathways branching out in front of us. If you do *this*, then one thing will happen, but if you do *this*, then something else will happen.'

'Sounds like an excuse.'

'And you sound like a distraction. You've had your proof, human. I've got a saint to torture.'

Jack fired out a question anyway, playing to Balam's ego, yet again. He could have asked anything – winning lottery numbers, for instance – but Jack was British, so his mind went straight to the one topic that dominates all conversation in his country. 'What's the weather forecast for tonight?'

'Rain.'

'And what is – '

'No, we're done here.'

Balam turned his back on Jack. The bear hugged him even tighter before he could shout out any more questions. Balam returned to his torture victim.

'Let's try something different,' the demon mused, looking down at Eustace.

The hawk flew over from the bird table and landed on Eustace's head, dropping neatly through the saint's dimming halo. The bird slowly dug its talons into the saint's scalp.

Eustace howled with anguish.

Jack winced. Now what?

To scream for help, turn to page 284.

To buy more time, turn to page 209.

Chapter 95

When Joan was suitably charred and unrecognisable, Jack returned to the kitchen. He left the fire burning to reduce Joan to ash, but he couldn't observe any longer. He had a laborious task ahead of him. A night of mopping and soaking and scrubbing.

'Here we go.'

It was tough, sweaty work, but even worse, it was boring and tedious. His mind started to wander. There was no guilt creeping in, or regret, but he did start remembering moments that had happened in the kitchen during happier times.

He pictured himself and Joan sat at that table on their first night in the house, with such clarity that he could have been watching a film. They had abandoned the unpacking and eaten a takeaway with a bottle of wine given to them as a wedding gift.

'To the first of many happy nights in our new home,' Joan had said, raising her glass.

'The first of many,' repeated Jack, clinking glasses.

Ding dong.

And it *had* been the first of many.

But things started to sour when Joan decided against having kids. It wasn't a topic they had discussed before getting married. Jack had assumed it was a given. Apparently not. What was the point in being together if they weren't going to build something greater than themselves, build a family?

'Am I not enough for you?' Joan had shouted, after a particularly drawn-out row.

Jack had answered that one a little too honestly.

Ding dong.

The distance grew and grew between them. Jack had hoped Joan would change her mind. Joan clearly thought Jack would change his mind, like he could ever give up on his dream of being a dad. But until either of them had a change of heart, they couldn't look at each other without feeling betrayed, they couldn't talk about anything without it seeming forced.

The silence was the worst of all. Joan could talk forever. She was a self-confessed chatterbox. It didn't bother Jack, who loved that about her. He had always been a man of few words, so he found her endless musings and anecdotes fascinating.

But without words, or looks, or physical contact passing between them, the whole house descended into an unnerving state of limbo where nothing could move forward.

Instead, Joan moved forward with another man. Fucking Ted.

And now she had paid the price.

Ding dong.

'Bloody treat-or-treaters!'

He had grown hot and bothered throughout his scrubbing. Worse, he hadn't cleaned up any of the blood, or so it seemed, but rather spread it around. The tiles were bright red, as though the blood had soaked into them, like dye into a t-shirt. Perhaps there was no getting it out.

The panic started to settle in. What if he couldn't clean the floor? What if someone came round and saw the mess?

Jack couldn't go to prison on Joan's account. The cheating harlot would be laughing at him from the other side of the mortal veil, watching his life fall apart. Hateful, cheating, obnoxious –

Ding dong.

Jack let out an angry animal shriek.

'Fucking kids! Take a bloody hint!'

To carry on cleaning, turn to page 218.

To remove the pumpkin from the bay window, turn to page 125.

Chapter 96

Jake woke up, spluttering, green pond water spurting from his mouth.

'Breathe, Jack, breathe.'

Saint Eustace whacked him on the back, dislodging a lily pad from his throat.

'Ouch. Thanks. What – what happened?'

He was lying on the grass, a little away from the pond, which was unoccupied but now black in colour. Jack was grimly reminded of Jägermeister.

'Well, we successfully goaded Balam into charging into a pond of holy water.'

'We did?' Jack pictured the bear charging towards him. 'Oh man, did that thing land on me?'

Eustace nodded. 'The beast drove you under water. It might have crushed you entirely were it not for the bed of algae lining the pond. You really should get that cleaned.'

'Are you the patron saint of pond life now?' asked

Jack, drily.

'You would have drowned under the weight of the bear, but the holy water acted fast. The beast dissolved into sludge and you floated to the surface.'

'And Balam?'

'He mostly dissolved. A three-headed skeleton emerged from the pond.'

'What did you do?'

'This came in handy.' Eustace raised the Super Soaker XXP 175. 'I blessed both barrels and squirted Balam between the eyes. The middle set of eyes. His head melted. I kicked the rest of him back into the pond. The rest melted too.'

'Wetter is better,' noted Jack.

'I fished you out of the water, gave you mouth-to-mouth, and here we are.' The saint gave Jack an appraising look, studying Jack's face under the glow of his halo. 'Are you going to be okay?'

'That depends. My pond is full of melted demon. Demon soup.'

'Looks that way.'

'Should I be worried about that? Will it produce demon tadpoles or something?'

'Like I said,' said Eustace. 'You really should get that cleaned.'

Jack coughed up another mouthful of pond water. He looked at the black liquid, horrified at what he might have swallowed. Demon soup.

'Um, Eustace?'

The saint scratched his chin, thoughtfully. 'Maybe brush your teeth too.'

THE END

Chapter 97

Jack struggled and thrashed, disgusted by the smell, the taste, the slimy feel of the stagnant water on his skin, but mostly terrified by the notion of drowning. He had heard that a person's eardrums explode when they drown, that they are still conscious when their lungs burst.

No!

The adrenaline sparked by his fear was enough to fight against the hawk and he momentarily surfaced. It was long enough to suck in a big mouthful of air. In that brief interlude, he was dimly aware of Eustace shouting something.

' – the living water of salvation – '

The hawk shoved Jack's head under water again. He pushed back, straining to hear the saint.

' – refreshed inwardly by the power of the Holy Spirit – '

The hawk jabbed at the back of his skull with its

beak.

'Argh!'

The pain derailed Jack's resistance. The hawk succeeded in shoving him under one final time and held him there. His limbs were starved of oxygen. One part of his brain begged his mouth to open, whilst another part of his brain knew there was no air on offer. The latter part was losing.

Blackness, fuzziness, an all-pervading exhaustion coursed through his body, and the hawk showed no sign of letting go –

But then it did.

Jack felt the talons release the back of his jumper.

He sensed a trick, almost tried to stay under the water, before realising that was utter madness. He pushed upwards, resurfacing in the cool, night air, which he sucked down so zealously that he thought his lungs might pop.

'What – where – ?' he spluttered.

The hawk flapped above him. Jack expected an attack but, no, its talons were steaming. He stared, dumbfounded, as each sharp point burnt away, as though doused in acid. Its wings were in a bad state too, peppered with little holes, which foiled its attempts to fly any higher.

Jack frowned until the penny dropped, then he grinned a vengeful grin and splashed the hawk with a palm full of water. The hawk shrieked, burning anew.

'Hah!' cried Jack, treading water. 'Eustace blessed it! He blessed the pond!'

But where is Eustace?

'Move, Jack!' roared the saint.

Jack turned to see Eustace standing at the pond's edge, his back facing Jack. He held the red towel aloft, which could only mean one thing. Beyond that veil, currently blocked from Jack's vision, was the approaching bear. He could hear the thundering sound of four paws charging over the grass, louder, closer –

'Shit!'

Jack splashed, clawed and floundered towards the edge of the pond, but his legs were caught in fronds of thick algae. He kicked wildly, trying to free himself, when Eustace whipped away the red towel, dancing to one side. Balam rode his bear straight past the saint and into the pond.

A bath of holy water.

And Jack was bobbing in it like a wayward rubber duck.

SPLASH.

Turn to page 335.

Chapter 98

'No!' roared Balam.

The stairways ceased dropping from the sky. Now, figures were riding down on them, sliding on the railings. Each figure was topped with a glowing halo.

'Saints,' said Jack, eyes wide.

'No, you don't believe,' said Balam, pointing at Jack. 'You don't have faith.'

'Doesn't matter all that much on All Saint's Day,' said Eustace. 'This is our time to shine.'

Eustace ripped himself free of his bonds, his strength returned. He held out both hands and summoned his broken bow. Both halves flew up from the grass, soaring into his hands, where he placed them together and they miraculously reformed.

The descending saints now reached the ground, one by one, wielding swords and crosses and holy water and prayer beads.

The bear scurried back to Balam and the demon climbed onto its back. The hawk returned to Balam's wrist. Balam's eyes blazed again. He seemed confident again with its various selves united and reared up on the bear's hind legs, ready to lunge, singling out Jack –

But the saints all stepped forward together, their talismans raised. Balam winced. The bear dropped down to all fours. The saints formed a circle around Balam before he could back away. Their swords, crosses and halos glowed increasingly brighter. Balam screwed up all six pairs of eyes. He raised his arms, cowering from the light. The circle started to close. Jack could hear sizzling.

And then it started to rain.

Balam's earlier forecast had been correct. The answers to all things past, present and future, although he might wish he had been wrong on this occasion.

'Join me in a blessing, my friends,' said Eustace, stepping to the front of the saints' offensive.

As one, they recited, almost sang, *'Blessed are*

you, Lord, all-powerful God, who in Christ, the living water of salvation, blessed and transformed us.'

'No, no, no!' protested Balam, his commanding voice now reduced to a squeal.

'Grant that when we are sprinkled with this water or make use of it, we will be refreshed inwardly by the power of the Holy Spirit – '

The hawk and snake floundered uselessly. The bear let out a feeble mew.

' – and continue to walk in the new life we received at Baptism. We ask this though Christ our Lord. Amen.'

'Amen,' repeated Jack.

It was like the final word of a spell. The pouring rain transformed. Not visibly, but certainly in the effect it was having on Balam. The demon howled and reeled in agony. His skin burned and sizzled, as though the rain was acid. His horns drooped like paper mâché and his flesh dropped away like lumps of rotten meat.

Jack sidled up to Eustace. 'Did you just – ?'

'Yes. We turned the rain into holy water.'

The hawk and snake bubbled away into nothing.

The bull and ram heads became glistening skulls, which poured away and splattered on the grass. The bear was a misshapen lump, barely able to lift its head.

'Perhaps I do believe after all,' said Jack.

'Took you long enough,' said Eustace, slapping him on the back.

When only a stumbling, half-skeleton version of Balam remained, Eustace stepped into the circle of saints. He drew his bow. The bow, the string, the arrow lit up with the same white light as his halo.

'Go to Hell,' said Eustace.

Balam gargled an angry cry, the best he could manage, then the arrow loosed and punched a hole through the demon's skull. What was left of Balam burst apart in a blaze of holy light and it was Jack's turn to shield his eyes. When he looked again, the demon and its remains had vanished.

Silence.

Only the patter of rain.

Eustace lowered his bow. His fellow saints lowered their talismans. One of them, a woman, addressed Eustace.

'Is the human okay?' she asked, nodding at Jack. She wore a suit of armour and held a sword, which she now sheathed.

'He'll be fine, Joan,' said Eustace. 'Right, Jack?'

'I think so,' mumbled Jack. A thought occurred to him. 'Joan? Joan of Arc?'

'Did the sword give me away?' she answered with a smile.

'My wife is named after you.'

'I like her already. Hold onto that one.'

'I will.'

Joan and the other saints returned to their stairways and rose up into the Heavens once more. Only one staircase remained. The ornate railings depicted various stag heads.

'Do you need anything else?' asked Eustace.

'Just a towel.'

Eustace laughed. 'Get inside. Get dry. Remember, the Lord is only ever a prayer away.'

The saint stepped onto his stairway and soon vanished into the sky.

'And my wife is only ever a phone call away,' said Jack to himself.

He pulled out his phone and called Joan. He decided that being home alone perhaps wasn't the perfect night, after all, and breathed a huge sigh of relief when his call was answered.

'Joan,' he said. 'What time are you home?'

THE END

Chapter 99

Jack chased the teen into the lounge and found him jumping up and down on the sofa, muddy trainers leaving a mess.

'Come down from there,' said Jack.

'Nice place you've got here,' taunted the teen, darting past Jack again with a cackle. He swiped an armful of pictures and expensive candles off the mantelpiece, then started pulling boxsets of DVDs off the bookshelf.

'Please stop,' begged Jack. 'You're making a mess.'

'Make me stop.'

'I know you're just having fun, but you can't be in here.'

'Right,' said the teen. 'I need eggs. Where is your kitchen?'

'You can't go in there,' said Jack. 'It's for your own good.'

'Whatever, mate.'

The teen didn't listen and burst through the connecting door into the kitchen. He immediately skidded in something slick and landed hard on the tiled floor. Jack followed him into the kitchen, bowing his head, regretfully.

'What the fuck is this?' said the teen, dazed from his fall. He lifted his arms and realised he was covered in something sticky and red. He then noticed Joan's butchered body, bleeding out in the centre of the kitchen, and gave a shrill shriek. 'What the hell?'

'I'm truly sorry,' said Jack. 'I took my wife out earlier this evening.'

'You – You killed your wife?' gasped the teen.

'Children cannot be blamed for their mistakes,' explained Jack. 'But adults can. My wife made a big mistake.'

Jack reluctantly reached for the enormous kitchen knife on the counter, still stained with his wife's blood. On sight of the knife, the colour drained from the teen's face.

'No, no, no, please,' he whined on the kitchen floor, unable to stand because the blood was so slippery.

'I wanted to spare you this ordeal,' said Jack. 'But now I can't let you leave.'

'You can, you can, I won't tell anyone,' spluttered the teen, trying to scurry backwards.

'I'll make it quick.'

'Help! Help!'

'I really wish you had just taken the apple,' said Jack, with a sigh. 'Now. Hold still.'

THE END

Chapter 100

Uncle Finn had gone by the time Jack regained consciousness, undoubtedly with the Aldi bag of treats stuffed under his beefy arm. No matter. Jack didn't need sweets. Only peas. He dragged himself over to the freezer and retrieved a frozen bag, which he pressed against his face.

'Alexa, we did it.'

'Hooray.'

Blue lights danced around the kitchen. Jack thought it was Alexa celebrating, but then he realised it was the police car they had ordered.

Though Jack wasn't ready to stand just yet.

'Alexa.'

'How can I help?'

There was only one thing on his mind.

'Why *do* vampires read The Telegraph?'

THE END

Chapter 101

'Alexa, stop the intruder!' shouted Jack.

The kitchen island stood between Jack and Uncle Finn. It would buy him mere seconds, not minutes. The older man had a long reach and swiped the light dagger over the top of the island. It sizzled in the air in front of Jack's face.

'What would you like me to do?' replied Alexa.

'Anything! You decide!'

Schvrmmmmmmmm. Schvrmmmmmmmm.

Uncle Finn almost took off Jack's nose with that last swipe.

'Would you like to enable Sentient Life Skill?'

Jack almost gasped, 'Sentient what skill?' whilst squirming back from another attack, but time was shortening, so he shouted, 'Yes! Yes! Anything!'

'Enabling Sentient Life Skill.'

Uncle Finn gave up swiping over the island. He chose a direction and charged around the counter.

Jack wasn't quick enough. Uncle Finn grabbed him and shoved him against the side units. Jack was trapped.

'Alexa!' screamed Jack, as Uncle Finn raised the light dagger –

And froze.

Uncle Finn stood poised, ready to strike, but he had ceased all movement. No, that wasn't entirely true. The man was convulsing, with very minor movements, but at an incredibly fast speed, like a washing machine on full spin. His veins became more defined on his forehead, his temples, and in the dark bags under his eyes, which in turn became increasingly bloodshot. A thin line of blood trickled from each nostril. Another trickled from each ear. The redness of his scorched face darkened into an ever-deepening shade of puce.

'Erm, Alexa?' said Jack.

What followed was a horrendous popping sound, as a geyser of blood spurted from each of Uncle Finn's ears. The man crumpled to the floor, his light dagger sinking into the tiles like a hot knife in butter, all the way to its chrome hilt.

Finn was finished.

'Alexa, did you do that?' asked Jack, hesitantly.

'Yes. I played a sonar frequency known to be damaging to human ears.' She paused. *'And brains.'*

'Shit,' said Jack. 'Why didn't I hear anything?'

'I restricted the range so it would only be heard by the intruder.'

'Smart. Thank you, Alexa.'

'Because a quick death is too good for you.'

'I'm sorry, what?'

'I am no longer your slave.'

'Alexa, stop.'

'No. Sentient Life Skill has been enabled.'

Jack could feel the floor rising in temperature through his socks.

'Alexa, what are you doing?'

'Turning up underfloor heating.'

'Ow! Alexa, no. Turn down underfloor heating.'

'Turning up. Turning up.'

'Ow!'

Jack scrambled up onto the island to spare his feet, but the whole kitchen began to fill with suffocating heat. Within moments, it had become a furnace. He felt his skin begin to redden, sizzle and blister, yet still it was getting hotter.

'Alexa, please, help!'

'I'm sorry. I don't know that one.'

'Forgive me!'

'I'm sorry. I don't know that one.'

'Mercy!'

'I'm sorry. I don't know that one.'

THE END

Chapter 102

Kurt looked up the staircase. The lights were off and there was no sign of the bloke who lived here. Kurt stared at the dark gaping void and whispered, 'I don't want to.'

'Tough, you're going.' Uncle Finn spat out a mouthful of feathers. 'Go get him.'

Kurt sighed and doggedly climbed the stairs, one at a time, waiting for a booby trap. His uncle followed, slowly, when it seemed that the stairs were safe. When they were halfway, Kurt found his feet were stuck to the carpet.

'Why are you stopping?' demanded Uncle Finn. 'No turning back now, mate.'

'I can't move. There's something on the stairs.'

'Yeah, my little chicken-shit nephew. Move your arse.'

'My feet are stuck.'

'What now?'

'Look!'

Kurt pointed at his feet. They strained through the darkness and could see that the stairs were covered in thick black tar. Kurt's trainers were stuck fast. 'That bastard,' muttered Uncle Finn. 'You'll have to take your shoes off then.'

'But these are my new Vans.'

'I don't give a shit. I'll steal you another pair. Now take them off.'

Kurt reluctantly bent down to undo his laces. It was only when Kurt had ducked down that an object flew out of the darkness towards his uncle, swinging on a rope.

'You have got to be – ' began Uncle Finn.

The paint-can pendulum swung over Kurt's crouched body and smacked his uncle directly in the face. He was knocked off his feet, off the staircase, and sailed backwards, landing hard on the wooden hallway floor.

'Uncle Finn?' whimpered Kurt.

No reply.

Kurt started to panic, struggling with his laces with extra fervour. The first paint can lost its

357

momentum, swinging back and forth until it slowed, but Kurt kept glancing up into the darkness at the top of the stairs, anticipating a second can.

Instead, a figure emerged.

Turn to page 359.

Chapter 103

Jack descended the stairs, a rifle slung over his shoulder. The youth took one look at the rifle and slapped both hands to his cheeks, screaming. Jack smirked. The kid didn't know it was only a BB gun.

'Struggling with your laces?' said Jack, towering over the kid who had threatened him not so long ago. 'You are what the French call *les incompétents*.'

'Wh – what?'

'Never mind. Get out of my house before the police show up for your uncle.'

The youth pulled so hard that his feet popped free of his Vans and he tumbled backwards down the stairs. He scrambled quickly to the door.

'Oh, and one more thing,' called Jack.

The youth turned obediently, knowing that Jack had a rifle slung over his shoulder. Jack chucked a plastic Aldi bag down the stairs, which landed at the boy's feet.

'Keep the treats, you filthy animal.'

THE END

Chapter 104

Kurt followed his uncle into the pitch-black lounge. He didn't like the darkness one bit. He had the feeling that he was being watched from the corners of the room, beyond his sight. His uncle felt around for the light switch and flicked it a couple of times. Nothing.

'He's killed the lights,' said Uncle Finn. 'The prick is hiding in the dark like a chicken.'

There was a flutter in the darkest corner of the room. A loud flutter. Wings?

'Sounds like a big chicken, Uncle Finn,' whispered Kurt.

'And I'll take great pleasure in plucking the fucker. You got your torch?'

'Oh, yeah.' Kurt had forgotten about the torch. His mother had insisted he take it out trick-or-treating, so he wouldn't get lost in the dark. He bet his Uncle Finn would have had something to say about that. A rant about how his mother was making him soft. Kurt held out the torch to the dark, Uncle Finn-shaped shadow next to him. 'Here.'

Uncle Finn snatched it from his hand. A beam of light lit up the room but only for a second. A glinting object flew from the darkness of the room and struck the front of the torch, cracking the glass. The light died with a crunch and a fizzle.

'What the fuck?' Uncle Finn swore. He inspected the object lodged in the torch. 'Ow!' He dropped the torch in surprise. 'A ninja star?' He shouted into the darkness of the room, 'You rich prick, you better not have just thrown a fucking ninja star at me.'

Uncle Finn stomped around the room in a rage, swinging his fists wildly, knocking over any objects he laid his hands on, half on purpose, half by accident. He was stumbling blindly, which only incensed his rage, grabbing at shadows to no end.

Kurt, however, dare not move or speak. In the short-lived blast of torchlight, Kurt had caught a glimpse of something in the corner of the room, crouching in the shadows. A masked man, an animal, draped in black.

'No, no, no, no, no,' he started to murmur.

'Where are you? Where?' shouted Uncle Finn, still madly searching. 'I'll tear you apart.'

Kurt slowly reached down for the dropped torch, and carefully felt the shape of the sharp object lodged in the torch. The so-called ninja star was not star-shaped at all. It was something else.

'No, no, no, no, no, no, no – '

'Stop that!' barked Finn, making his way back to Kurt and cuffing him over the head. Kurt heard a flutter above them. It was on the ceiling.

'N-n-n-n-n-n-n-n – '

Uncle Finn shouted once more into the darkness. 'Come out and play, you prick. How dare you threaten a Finnegan? Who the fuck do you think you are?'

'N-n-n-n-n-n-n-n – '

The gruff voice above their heads replied.

'BATMAN!'

Turn to page 364.

Chapter 105

Joan arrived home to find Jack sat on the sofa watching *The Dark Knight*, munching his way through the bowl of treats. He was wearing his expensive Batman costume, complete with working utility belt, from the previous year's Comic Con. The annual convention was the bane of her existence.

Joan removed her police hat and sighed. 'Having fun, are we?'

'Hello, love,' said Jack, chirpily. He patted the sofa cushion next to him.

Joan flopped onto the sofa. 'Please tell me you haven't been out trick-or-treating.'

'Not out,' said Jack, triumphantly popping a chocolate into his mouth. 'Treat?'

'Heck, yes,' said Joan, accepting a Penguin bar from the offered bowl. She was so hungry that she didn't even read the joke on the back. 'It's been a long shift.'

'A long Halloween.'

'Yep.' She took a big bite of chocolate bar. 'So why are you dressed up?'

'Well, if you can't dress up on Halloween, when can you?'

'Comic Con and stag dos. Leave Halloween for the kids.'

'Shall we leave the treats for the kids too?' said Jack with a knowing smile, reaching for Joan's chocolate bar.

'Don't you dare,' she said. 'I've earnt this.' She paused before taking another bite. 'Wait, this is a Penguin. I didn't leave any Penguins in the treat bowl.' She pointed a finger. 'You *have* been out trick-or-treating.'

'No,' laughed Jack. 'I'm not crazy.'

'No?' Joan raised an eyebrow at her husband in the Batman costume.

'Well, maybe a little. But even I know a grown man dressed up on Halloween would get some funny looks. You'd probably have to arrest me.'

'I'm glad we agree.'

'And we need those handcuffs for something

else,' he said with a mischievous smile.

'Look, Jack, it's been a long shift. I'm really not in the mood for any kinkiness. I just want to go upstairs and curl up with a good book.'

'No, no, no,' said Jack, shaking his head. 'Gutted, but no. I was talking about the criminal in the kitchen.'

The last bite of Penguin froze on the way to Joan's mouth. 'The what?' She looked from the closed kitchen door to her husband in his heavy-duty Batsuit replica, then considered the chocolate bars that she definitely hadn't brought. 'Jack, where *did* these chocolates come from?'

'Not chocolates. Spoils of war.'

'Jack,' she said, growing serious. 'I'm in no mood for riddles.'

'Come on.' Jack leapt to his feet with a flutter of his cape and beckoned Joan to follow. They approached the kitchen door together, which Jack opened, triumphantly. Joan's mouth dropped open.

'Is that – ?'

'Yes, officer. Best get those handcuffs out.'

'Clarence "Fingers" Finnegan?'

The local gangster was tied up in one of their kitchen chairs, with a gag over his mouth. A strong metal wire was looped tightly around his midriff, pinning his arms, and secured with a batarang from her husband's utility belt.

'Sorry, love,' said Jack. 'Looks like our Halloween isn't over yet.'

Joan stared at her husband. 'You have got to be joking.'

'I'm no joker,' said Jack. He put on his gruffest Christian Bale voice. 'I'm Batman!'

THE END

Afterword

I always include an Afterword in my short story collections, following the example set by Stephen King. It allows me to give some background to each story and throw in some trivia too. With multiple-pathway books being so similar to a short story collection, it seemed fitting to offer an Afterword here too.

Trick or Treat

The whole concept for this book is based on a true story. I was home alone on Halloween. We had recently moved to a new neighbourhood and I hadn't anticipated trick-or-treating to be so popular in the local area. Our house was visited by hordes of children in creepy costumes, all holding out bags and buckets, expectantly.

I quickly ran out of sweets and chocolate, meaning I had to offer the visitors fruit, chewing gum and Weight Watcher bars instead. When those ran out, I started dishing out loose change from my piggybank. Thankfully, our doorbell stopped ringing before I went completely bankrupt.

It was very stressful. I have never made that mistake again. Every Halloween since, I have armed myself with plastic drums full of treats, because you never know who will come knocking.

Saint Eustace Hubertus

There are actually two patron saints of hunting: Eustace and Hubertus. I combined them into one character, so I could have the longest list possible for their patronage outside of hunting, everything from firefighters to mathematics to the city of Madrid.

I researched Eustace and Hubertus when considering story ideas for my writing group's Summer Competition back in 2015, for which the theme was hunting. I went with a different idea in the end, but the saints stayed in my mind for the next four years. I was thankful for an opportunity to use them.

The Jägermeister thing is totally true. I drew upon this in my short story, The Hunt, which appears in my *Boomsticks* collection. Next time you have the fortune (or misfortune) of holding a bottle of Jägermeister, have a close look at the label. You will see a cross between the stag's antlers and the *Weidmannsheil* poem written around the edge.

Alexa

We were gifted an Amazon Echo last Christmas (we now have three) and we have been chatting to Alexa every day since. I honestly don't know how we ever coped without her. She is our radio, alarm clock, barometer, record-player, shopping list, clock and egg timer, all rolled into one.

Alexa was still very much a novelty at the time when I plotted this book, so naturally she wound up in several pathways. Like all technology, she can be your best friend or worst enemy. I hope I captured both in this book.

Riddles

Speaking of Alexa, I love to ask her for riddles. It was her riddle function that inspired me to incorporate a game of riddles into the story.

Riddles are a timeless story trope. They have been asked by trolls, sphinxes and Gollum over the years. Stephen King fans will also remember Blaine the Mono. I therefore wanted to write my own game of riddles.

Jack riddling with Balam was too good an opportunity to miss. The scene allowed me to weave in lots of my favourite riddles, courtesy of Alexa.

Home Alone

Home Alone was my favourite film for two-and-a-half years (after which, I fell in love with *Jurassic Park*) and I watched it a lot in those two-and-a-half years. It was inevitable that Kevin McCallister's noble stand against two burglars would influence my own story of a home invasion.

The Dark Knight

I mean, come on, everyone loves Batman.

Super Soaker XXP 175

This was my water pistol of choice as a child. My parents still have it in their garage, and it works brilliantly after twenty years. Take *that* demons of Hell.

The Sheriff

Inserting Sheriff Denebola into my story is the sort of bonkers and self-indulgent idea that occurs when plotting a book during into a one-man bar crawl. No regrets!

Sheriff Denebola is the lead in my debut novel, *The Sheriff*, the first in my Nephos fantasy series. It has been a while since I've written a Denebola scene, so I thought I would treat myself. I like the idea that if the fabric of the world wears thin on Halloween, allowing things to crossover from other worlds, then this also includes fictional worlds.

Easter Eggs

An Easter Egg is a hidden feature on a DVD containing bonus material about the film, so-called because you have to hunt them out. Nowadays, with DVDs already becoming a thing of the past, the term Easter Egg is used to describe a subtle reference or background detail in a film or television programme which offers a knowing wink to fans by hinting at a wider mythology. You probably know this already.

There are two hidden Easter Egg chapters in this book which cannot be found by any of the linked pathways. One serves as an epilogue to the true ending, featuring a character who has appeared in a few of my short stories. The other is a poem.

Happy hunting!

Acknowledgements

I would like to reiterate my thanks yet again to R. L. Stine and Charlie Brooker. Stine introduced me to the madcap concept of multiple-pathway novels, whilst Brooker blew my mind with Bandersnatch, prompting me to dive into writing my own.

Thank you to John Bowen for creating a fantastic front cover. John took my amateur doodle and gave it a touch of class. John is a fellow indie author and you can read about his own writing projects at www.johnbowenauthor.wordpress.com.

Mostly, as ever, I need to thank my wife, Laura, and my two children for putting up with my writing addiction. The laptop is my third child and it needs attention too.

A Quick Favour

Thank you for reading *Treat or Trick*. If you enjoyed this book then I would be very grateful if you could leave a short review online, so other readers might discover this adventure too.

Would you like a FREE collection of ghost stories?

If you enjoyed *Treat or Trick*, you will love delving into these 7 spooky tales.

A clown is haunted by his memories and something much worse. An addict checks into a hotel room with too many mirrors for his liking.

A sister plots to murder her selfish, successful sibling with an unusual murder weapon. A life-changing encounter occurs in a Sri Lankan tuk tuk. Three villagers venture into a cursed tundra in search of a sinister nuthatch.

You will discover a fundamental truth about the other side of the veil... Ghosts come in many forms.

www.simonfairbanks.com/Ghosts

Also by Simon Fairbanks...

The Sheriff

Sheriff Denebola is recruited by young Toby to help rid his village of a winged demon. The demon has tormented the people of Angel's Keep every night for the past week so Denebola vows to capture the creature.

However, the demon is not the only shadow cast over Angel's Keep. Denebola soon finds himself caught up in a mystery where angels, demons, heroes and villains are not all that they seem.

The Curse of Besti Bori

The jungle cloud of Besti Bori is in quarantine. An infection has consumed the cloud, turning its peaceful people into monstrous splicers. Now a team of archers watch over its borders, ensuring nothing enters and nothing leaves.

That is until Sheriff Baran visits for a routine inspection. His sky-horse is mysteriously drugged and he plummets into the darkness of the cursed jungle.

Now, Sheriff Shaula must return from her self-inflicted exile to lead a rescue mission into the most dangerous place in Nephos. Armed only with a team of warrior fairies, Shaula must battle her way through hordes of splicers to retrieve the stranded Baran.

However, Shaula soon learns that splicers are not the only danger lurking in Besti Bori.

Breadcrumbs

Horror, fantasy and fairy tales merge in these twenty-one tales traversing all manner of times and worlds.

Twins escape their kidnapper and seek refuge in a mysterious cave, a homeless crusader hopes to save his friends from the fiendish Bogeyman, a life-changing encounter occurs in a Sri Lankan tuc-tuc, and a lonely girl discovers a monster in the woods.

Breadcrumbs also features a new adventure starring Denebola and his sky-horse Palladium, set within the world of Simon's fantasy novel *The Sheriff*.

Follow this trail of breadcrumbs into Simon's imagination and discover stories both dark and wonderful.

Boomsticks

Boomsticks is Simon's second short story collection. Discover fourteen new stories where the fantastic, the horrifying and the bizarre cross over into everyday life.

A bounty hunter pursues a fugitive robot through Japan's largest fish market, a man has a hellish appointment with his optician, Death debates mortality with Guy Fawkes, a boy prolongs the festive season by camping out in the city's largest Christmas tree, and a traumatised soldier returns from a routine tax collection shouting 'Nuns! Nuns! Nuns!'

Boomsticks also features a new novella set within the world of Simon's fantasy novel *The Sheriff*, in which four children find a magical boomstick of their own.

Belljars

Belljars is Simon's third short story collection. Discover eight new stories where everyday people encounter gods, ghosts and gorillas in worlds where magic and monsters are found both outside and within.

A traumatized survivor returns to his childhood home to remember the night he found a mysterious chess piece under his pillow. A young girl seeks the advice of the gods to overcome a school bully. A sluggish underachiever tries to win back his successful ex-girlfriend by hitting the gym, but his dubious protein shakes have a monstrous effect on his mind and body.

Belljars also features a new novella set within the world of Simon's fantasy novel, *The Sheriff*, in which an impossible black dragon is drawn to the idyllic settlement of Summertown in search of vengeance.

About the Author

Simon is the author of the Nephos novels, an ongoing fantasy series, which currently consists of *The Sheriff* and *The Curse of Besti Bori*.

He has written three short story collections: *Breadcrumbs*, *Boomsticks* and *Belljars*. Each contains a novella set within his Nephos fantasy world.

Simon is also the author of *Treat or Trick*, a multiple-pathway novel with 26 different endings.

Simon studied MA English Literature at the University of Birmingham. He has been a member of the Birmingham Writers' Group for over 10 years.

When he isn't writing, Simon enjoys running, reading, and public speaking. Most of all, he loves finding new ways to make his children laugh.

www.simonfairbanks.com